GOWRIE ADVENTURE

GOWRIE ADVENTURE

M. Whiteford

REX COLLINGS LONDON 1979

First published in Great Britain by
Rex Collings Ltd
69 Marylebone High Street, London W1

© M. Whiteford 1979

ISBN 0860 36 1068

Typesetting by Malvern Typesetting Services Ltd
Printed in Great Britain by
Billing & Sons Ltd
London, Guildford and Worcester

Contents

Arrival

It was really dark by the time the taxi stopped in the car park at the foot of Gowrie Brae. The children were having to get out there and walk the last quarter-mile to the cottage because there was no road for a car beyond that point.

'Mrs Wood's expecting you, isn't she?' enquired Mr Macdougall as he unloaded their bags from the boot.

'Oh yes,' John assured him. 'It's all fixed. She'll have the house open and the fire on.'

'And our beds made,' added Robbie hopefully.

'See,' said Jandy, pointing to where a welcome twinkle shone from a window near the end of the line of cottages that made up Gowrie. 'That's our light there!'

She shivered a little as a sudden cool breeze sprang up. Mr Macdougall noticed this and hurried to take out the last of the baggage.

'That's the lot then,' he said heartily. 'Careful as you go now!'

Now they needed to contain their excitement no longer. Staying only to thank Mr Macdougall for his kindness—he would be sending the taxi bill to their father—they set off as fast as their various burdens would allow them towards No. 63.

Usually the first walk of the holidays along the 'bankie' took about an hour, for the children had to stop every now and then to greet old friends who were always glad to see them. There were the Woods at the shop, the Johnstons at the jetty, Mr MacRae the lobsterman and a dozen other old

1

inhabitants who were usually sunning themselves at their cottage doors or, in wet weather, sitting at their windows watching the summer visitors passing by.

But this was October, not July, and the villagers were more likely to be gathered around their firesides, watching television than to be looking out into the darkness on the off-chance of seeing a passer-by at that time. So there were no people to hold up the children's progress.

In summer too, there were the other old friends, the familiar sights and well-loved landmarks which cried out to be acknowledged just as compellingly as did the humans. Each of the Turnbulls had his or her own favourite spot. Robbie, for instance, always had to run the full length of the jetty just to get the panorama of the village which could only be had from there; Jandy, on the other hand, liked to stand for a few minutes at the letter-box set in the ruined gable of No. 40 and to look back for her first view of Porterfield tumbling picturesquely down its gully across the bay. The others, too, even Mum and Dad, had their own private rituals without which no arrival in Gowrie was complete.

But on this dark October night there were no views to be seen and therefore no opportunities to indulge in the usual ceremonials.

However none of these things were in the minds of Hamish or Shona Turnbull as they raced to be first at the cottage that evening. Well, perhaps I'm doing Hamish an injustice but he certainly never had the reputation of being a dog with a mind much above his stomach.

'It's a mercy,' thought Shona, 'that it *is* dark for I'd hate people to see me like this!'

And certainly she was being dragged along by the Scottie at a rate which would have affronted her had the evening been light and the neighbours watching. Straight along the path they ran, risking disaster on the uneven surface a dozen

2

times, over the plank bridge across the burn which divides Wester from Easter Gowrie, their feet ringing as they went and on—right up to the cheerful light and open door of No. 63—and then directly in without ceremony and over to the corner where, wonder of wonders! sat a succulent bowl of dog's dinner.

Mrs Wood rose from her seat by the fire with a smile.

'I heard the taxi on the brae,' she told Shona, 'and I knew his lordship here would be first off the mark!'

'He's a rude greedy thing,' said Shona as severely as she could, amid panting. 'He nearly pulled me off my feet out there and now he hasn't even stopped to thank you for getting his dinner!'

Hamish took her tone, as he took most things, simply as an encouragement to eat up even faster and he was not in the least offended.

The other three made their way along more sedately, partly because there was no ravenous dog to urge them on but mainly because of their bundles and packages. John was lugging the big hold-all with all their spare clothes, Jandy carried a large shopping bag full of food for the weekend and Robbie had—for the first few minutes at least—the unwieldy cat-basket through the wired window of which came an incessant, piteous miaowing from the affronted Tibby.

'Can I let her out now?' pleaded Robbie, after about five steps with this cumbersome load. 'Tibby'll know her way from here all right.'

'I think it should be okay,' said Jandy. 'Don't you John? There aren't likely to be any dogs around at this time.'

John agreed and so the protesting cat was liberated. Then it was a simple matter to leave the basket on one of the luggage barrows which were all lined up in the open space near the first houses.

'We'll collect it tomorrow,' John reassured his little

brother. 'Tibby won't need it again till we're on the way home.'

'I wish we could take our barrow,' remarked Jandy longingly, 'but I suppose it would be more bother than it's worth in the dark.'

'Dangerous too,' agreed her brother. 'You know how these things can run away with you even in broad daylight. We'd probably end up down on the shore with it if we tried taking it tonight.'

They fell silent after that as the village lamps were few and far between and they needed all their concentration for the path but even so it was not long until they too arrived at the cottage.

They crowded into the living-room, filling it with their chatter and laughter—and their belongings. Anoraks and scarves were cast off and heavy shoes thankfully discarded in favour of the sneakers which stood in a row in the corner. These last were the cause of much hilarity. Since more than a year had passed since they had last been at the cottage, all four children had of course grown a lot in the meantime. So now Robbie had to wear Shona's old sneakers, Shona needed Jandy's, Jandy—John's and John, his father's.

Robbie surveyed his old shoes, now of use to no-one.

'These might do for Hamish,' he said thoughtfully. 'It seems a pity to waste them.'

'Well he'd certainly like to chew them!' laughed Mrs Wood. 'But come on over and have something to chew yourself. John and Jandy, I'd just like a wee word with you first.'

She ushered the two young ones over to the table where they sat waiting expectantly for the food to arrive. Meanwhile Mrs Wood discussed the weekend's arrangements with the older children.

'I'm not going to interfere with your housekeeping, Jandy,' she said, 'for I know you're well able to cope but

4

remember to pop in and ask if you run short of anything. I've just left your tea tonight because I knew you'd be tired after your journey.'

This news was a great relief to Jandy. She had been looking forward to being in charge of the catering for this weekend and was beginning to see all her grand plans coming to ruin if Mrs Wood had wanted to be too helpful.

'Thank you very much,' she said. 'It's lovely to find every-thing waiting ready for us tonight but I hope I'll not have to bother you too much later.'

'Think nothing of it, my dear,' said Mrs Wood. 'It's grand to have some young life about the place at this time of year for a change. Gowrie's an awful quiet-like place in the winter.

'Now I'll away and leave you in peace. Oh, by the way John, I'm going up the hill to sit with Mrs Grant at the farm tonight and tomorrow evening. Donald's away at a meeting in Aberdeen and she finds the evenings a bit long when she's on her own. I'll not be late back but just in case you need any help during the evening, I'll leave word at the shop that you've arrived.'

John thanked her and saw her back next-door to her own house. She was an old friend and a good one but she did tend to rattle on a bit! Then John came back eagerly to No. 63 and his long-awaited meal.

He found Jandy busying herself happily at the cooker, making a quite unnecessary clatter with pots and spoons. The two youngsters were already tucking in happily to bowls of steaming broth. To follow, there were hot sausage rolls, baked beans and potato crisps. There were also plenty of warm rolls and biscuits and there was Coke to drink—and tea for the older Turnbulls.

'Oh, this is the life,' sighed John contentedly, leaning back at last after more than half an hour of solid eating.

5

'Why can't we always eat like this?'

'I do,' said Robbie happily, 'but it's even nicer here because of the noise of the sea outside.'

It was now quite late and much too dark to think of going out. All four children helped to clear the table and then for a while made a pretence of reading or doing a jigsaw puzzle but none of them seemed to have any real heart for what they were doing. Yet bed still seemed an anti-climax.

Then Robbie yawned and announced, 'Before I go to bed I'd like to hear the story of Alec Johnston.'

The Story of Alec Johnston

Now there were two Gowrie stories that the children never tired of hearing and there was always someone willing to oblige them.

One was the tale of the Big Storm of 1953. That was the year when great floods devastated many parts of Europe, including Holland and the South of England. Less publicized but more real to the people of North-East Scotland at that time was the week of freak waves driven by gales of unusual force which assaulted, among other places, the village of Gowrie. The culmination of that dreadful week was a night of terror when in a matter of hours several houses were literally swept away into the sea.

As regular visitors to the village the Turnbulls had heard that story many times from people who had actually lived through the experience. There were no human casualties in the disaster but to hear an eye-witness account of it was enough to send shivers up and down the spine and to make even the least imaginative listener look with more respect on the sea thereafter.

More romantic, however, because it happened so long ago and therefore could be embroidered in the telling without fear of contradiction, was the story of Alec Johnston.

As the eldest of the family, John was looked upon as the authority on this one in the Turnbull household. He had heard the story more often than anyone else, after all, and by now he had really made it his own. He was always ready to re-tell it to the others, putting in extra details from his fertile imagination each time.

The best of it was that the basic story was true.

Robbie was especially fond of it and often asked to hear it at bedtime. It seemed an appropriate way to round off this first holiday evening when they were all too tired to do anything very active and so once more John prepared to oblige.

'Okay,' he said. 'Are you sitting comfortably? Then I'll begin.'

The others giggled and settled themselves into suitable positions for listening. This meant that Robbie curled up into as nearly a round ball as human shape could contrive, Shona tucked her feet up elegantly and propped her chin in her cupped hands, while Jandy flopped cross-legged on the floor.

'It all happened many years ago,' began John, 'in the year 1746, to be exact, when terrible things were being done in the Highlands of Scotland. This was because Bonnie Prince Charlie and his followers had just been defeated at the Battle of Culloden and they were now being hunted down by their enemies.

'They managed to get the Prince away to safety in France but the rest of the Jacobites were hounded by the cruel troops of Butcher Cumberland, the King's general.'

7

'That was the English,' whispered Shona, who was a bit of a Scottish Nationalist. The remark was meant for Robbie's ears but it was Jandy who reacted.

'You're wrong, you know,' she said. 'There were plenty of Scots on the King's side and the Lowlanders were just as much against the Highlanders as the English were. Isn't that right, John?'

'Yes,' admitted her brother, 'but I wish you'd both shut up and let me tell my own story.' He gave his sisters a disapproving glare and then, feeling that they were suitably squashed, continued.

'Without their leader, the Jacobites had no-one to give them orders or organize them to fight back and all they could do was to go into hiding or try to make for their homes.

'It wasn't only the soldiers on the Jacobite side who suffered either—many women and children were put to the sword just because their clan was loyal to the Prince.

'Now at this time there was no Gowrie and not even any Porterfield. The only buildings around the bay here were a couple of fishermen's huts and old St Colm's Church up there on the hill.'

'This is the good bit now,' whispered Robbie, leaning over to nudge Shona.

In response to this encouragement John lowered his voice dramatically and fixed his eye on the delighted Robbie who wriggled with pleasure.

'One day in Autumn, when a cold mist was rolling in from the sea, shrouding the top of Gowrie Head so that nothing could be seen up there and keeping everyone inside their houses if they could possibly avoid going out, the fisherfolk were surprised to see a young woman with a baby wrapped in a tartan shawl in her arms, coming staggering and stumbling down Gowrie Brae. Of course, this was in the days before there were proper roads and the ground was very rough and uneven. This plus the fact that the poor woman was so weak with exhaustion made her nearly fall several times until at last she did collapse, down on the shore.

'She was deathly pale and the fishermen who hurried over to help her felt sure that she had not long to live. They took the baby away to care for it along with their own children and the woman was carried into one of their huts where she could at least die in peace. But to everyone's surprise she did not die. Instead, when she had had a few days' rest, she began to recover and soon she was asking for her baby. There was only one problem: no-one could find out the woman's story because she could only speak Gaelic while the local people only spoke English.

'It was months before they learnt enough of one another's languages to understand each other and when at last they did the woman's story horrified them so much that they wished they had not asked her to tell it at all.

'The woman was Mary Johnston and she had lived in a little cottage in a glen somewhere among the mountains. When the Prince raised his standard at Glenfinnan, her clan was one of the first to rise and follow him. Her husband was one of the first of his clan to go. She was proud of him for this even though it meant that she was left with six children and her husband's old parents to look after on her own. Still, she managed to keep things going somehow and she kept telling herself that she had only to wait till the Jacobites were victorious and then everything would turn out well for the Highlanders.'

'But they didn't win,' said Shona mournfully.

'No, they didn't. They were soundly defeated and from then on it was every man for himself. The Government troops were given complete freedom to steal and destroy and kill anywhere on Jacobite land.

'One day, when Mary Johnston was out at the peat-cutting with her baby, they came to her cottage and she returned home to find her house a smoking ruin and her children and the old folks all murdered.

'She nearly went mad with the shock and just ran away, not knowing where she was going. The next thing she remembered was coming to on Gowrie beach with the fishermen bending over her.

'Through time Mary became accepted as one of the community and they built a house for her and the baby. After a while some more of her people who had suffered as Jacobites too came to join her and so gradually the village grew.'

'And the baby was Alec Johnston,' cried Robbie.

'Yes, and he was your great-great-great- I don't know how many times great-grandfather,' finished John.

They all sighed and sat back, thinking with satisfaction over the familiar story but by now Robbie's head was drooping and he was easily persuaded to go off to bed accompanied by an equally drowsy Tibby. Soon Shona hustled a sleepy Hamish after him.

Jandy and John sat on in the living-room for a while savouring their freedom but by ten o'clock they too had succumbed to the effects of their busy day. So they went off to bed too.

Friday Night

As they parted for their separate rooms at the top of the stairs, John remarked to his sister, 'You know, I'll not really be surprised if I wake up tomorrow and find I'm back in Edinburgh after all. There was a jinx on this holiday from the start and I never really expected it to come off in the end.'

'I know,' agreed Jandy. 'It was nearly the holiday that never was. Still, if you want to be sure that you really are here, just lie and listen to the sound of the waves. You don't get that in Edinburgh!'

Despite their tiredness, or perhaps because of it, neither Jandy nor John fell asleep immediately. In the other bed in his room John could hear Robbie making comfortable little sleeping noises but his own mind was too busy going over the events of the past few weeks to rest just yet.

'How many times were our arrangements upset this year, I wonder,' he thought. 'I must just count.'

They really had had a series of disasters that summer. First of all, Robbie took measles just on the eve of the original holiday date and that had to be put back by a month. Then when the invalid was more or less restored to normal and holiday fever was reaching a climax again, the family car was badly damaged in an accident and the formalities for settling the insurance claim took so long that the matter was still being negotiated the week that the school vacation ended.

'What a return to school that was!' thought John, remembering how, as all his friends were exchanging holiday reminiscences he who was usually the most vociferous on these occasions had sat silent, hoping nobody would notice.

That would of course have been only a very temporary embarrassment to most people—for how many people never even have a holiday at all?—but John was not like that. He

11

took his holidays seriously and felt he could not face a whole boring year of routine without having had the chance to recharge his batteries in his beloved Gowrie.

'Edinburgh's all right,' he would tell anyone who would listen. 'I mean, it's fine for everyday living but my roots are in Gowrie and that's where I feel I really belong.'

The family connections with the village were certainly of long enough duration. Mrs Turnbull's mother, and many earlier generations too, had been born in the very No. 63 where the children were now staying and although she had long since moved away from the area the ownership of the cottage remained with the family.

The idea of making up for the earlier disappointments by spending the October mid-term week up North for once had come from Dad. He realized how seriously the children had taken the loss of their regular visit. Unfortunately it was Dad too who had to go to an important conference this very weekend and so was missing the first few days of even this short break. Mrs Turnbull had felt in duty bound to accompany her husband to the meeting because that was expected of wives in his firm. So once more gloom had descended.

Then John surprised them all, and himself too, by volunteering to take the younger members up North ahead of their parents.

'After all,' he pointed out, 'in the old days people of my age would have left school and would have been working. So surely I can be trusted to manage that lot.'

'It shows how desperate he must be to get away,' Mr Turnbull remarked privately to his wife on the evening the suggestion was made, for it was certainly not a typical gesture from the impractical John. 'Still, it might be the making of him to take on a bit of responsibility.'

Mrs Turnbull agreed but all the same she went quietly ahead and phoned Mrs Wood in Gowrie so that there would be someone available in case of emergency. She preferred to be safe rather than sorry.

'Oh well,' John told himself as he went over these events in his mind, 'we're here at last and that's the main thing. Tomorrow I start to make up for lost time.'

He turned to arrange his duvet more comfortably around himself while he thought what he would do next day but somehow his plans got no further than that stage, for at last the soothing lilt of the water lapping on the beach lulled John to sleep and he did not stir again till morning.

Next door Jandy too lay awake for a time but she was planning for the future, not thinking over the past. She had been as bitterly disappointed at all the ruined plans as John but in her case the present arrangement was a positive improvement on the original, not just a poor substitute.

She was as much of a doer as her brother was a dreamer. The trouble was that she did not have the scope to do what she wanted at home. Her passion was for cookery and nothing gave her greater pleasure than peeling potatoes, slicing onions, weighing out flour and measuring spoonfuls of this and that. The trouble was that she was so enthusiastic about her hobby that she was apt to monopolize the entire kitchen at home when she indulged in it and this led to ill-feeling.

But no-one could object to what she did this weekend for she was in sole charge of the catering until Mum and Dad joined them.

'Chief cook and bottle-washer you'll be, Jandy,' Dad had said, 'and don't you let the rest of them forget it. Cut down their rations if there's any insubordination.'

So Jandy lay in bed this first holiday night going over her menus.

'Tomorrow,' she planned, 'we'll have an omelette—a Spanish one with all sorts of bits and pieces in it. Maybe I

13

could get some chips in Porterfield to go with it. Then on Sunday I'll open that big tin of hamburgers and we'll have friend onions and hamburger rolls . . .'

And so her thoughts ran on to become merged at last in contented dreams.

Shona, Robbie and the two pets had long been asleep by now, each wrapped in his or her own private dreamworld. To Robbie, bed was for sleeping in and he would have considered it a waste of good sleeping time to lie and think. Shona was quite worn out with the strain of worrying about the behaviour of Hamish on his first train journey and though he had in fact been a model of decorum and had given no cause for complaint at all the stress had taken its toll.

'He was a real credit to us today,' was all she had time to think before sleep overcame her.

Now only the ceaseless murmuring of the sea-waves outside as they eddied now and again round the rocks on the shore-line and the occasional cry of a wakeful sea-bird disturbed the peace of the October night.

So all Gowrie slept.

Saturday: The Anniversary Concert

Next morning Jandy awoke to a familiar Gowrie sound and it had a familiar effect on her.

'That's Tibby miaowing outside the window, asking to be let in,' was her first thought. Then as she gathered her wits together preparatory to opening the window for the cat she realized, as she had done so often before, that she was back

14

in Gowrie and that the cat-like noise was made by a hungry sea-gull.

The gulls were one of the minor delights of the holidays. Each cottage in the village had its resident bird which guarded its own territory jealously. The Turnbulls often wondered what the birds did for food when they were not there to throw out scraps. Perhaps there was always some other kind-hearted visitor ready to take pity on them. At any rate, as soon as No. 63 was occupied each summer the stretch of ground between their front door and the beach was haunted by a large, haughty sea-gull and his much meeker wife. His name, according to Robbie and Shona at least, was George and while he was around no other bird except for the odd sparrow dared show so much as a feather there.

What had roused Jandy on this first holiday morning was the sound of George announcing that he was ready for his breakfast. She sighed and, rubbing her eyes, rolled over to reach for her watch which she always kept on the bedside table.

'Eight o'clock,' she murmured. 'That's a bit early for the first day of the holidays!'

Another impatient squawk from outside seemed to contradict her thoughts and as usual her conscience prevented her from taking the last forty winks she desired so much.

'Oh all right you greedy bird! I'm coming,' she said.

'What was that?' came a sleepy voice from the other bed and Shona's tousled head popped up from among the blankets with a look of enquiry.

'I'm just promising George that his breakfast is coming,' said Jandy, 'but there's no need for you to get up yet. It's only eight o'clock.'

'I'll have to get up if you do,' replied Shona. 'Hamish will expect to get out first thing and I wouldn't like to disappoint him on his holidays.'

She had hardly got beyond the word 'out' when there was a furious battering at their bedroom door. At some point during the night, Hamish had had to be ejected for prowling around the room and sneezing while the girls were trying to sleep and he had spent the night on the landing. Now he was demanding reinstatement.

This had an instant effect on Shona. She hopped quickly out of bed and over she ran to open the door.

'Now be quiet, Hamish,' she admonished, 'and if you're good we'll go for a walk.'

The two girls dressed quickly and in ten minutes they were hurrying downstairs.

Shona immediately made for the front door.

'Oh come and see what a lovely day it is, Jandy!' she cried. 'Just look at the sparkle on the water.'

Jandy joined her sister to stand gazing out over the sea.

'Thank goodness it's sunny,' she said. 'I was worried in case we'd have a week of bad weather because it's so late in the season.'

Even in summer, days like this one happened rarely in Gowrie. The sun was brilliant and all the muted colours of the Autumn took on a new radiance under its influence. Opposite No. 63, the headland beyond Porterfield glowed a deep purple with a scatter of bright, green fields on top and it was decked around its fringes with bracken of many shades of gold ranging from the palest to the deepest, rich tones. The old buildings of St Colm's Church on top looked very near in the clear morning light and not half so sinister as usual.

The upper houses in Porterfield itself also caught the sunlight and this brought out a surprising amount of detail even at such a distance.

'I think that's Nurse Troup,' cried Shona, screwing up her eyes and pointing to where a solitary figure on a bicycle could be seen pedalling down the almost vertical slope of Porterfield's main street. 'You would think she would walk that bit. She'll end up in the harbour!'

'Not a bit,' returned Jandy. 'She knows what she's doing all right.'

Once, in a flight of fancy unusual for her, Jandy had confided to her brother, 'I think two giants must have built these places. One poured Porterfield out of a jug so that it just filled that hollow in the hill and the houses landed any old how but the other squeezed Gowrie out of a tube so that it fitted exactly into the strip along the shore.'

John had hooted with laughter at this fantasy but Shona was enchanted with the idea. Certainly Gowrie could have been the work of a very neat-fingered giant. It is built on such a narrow ledge between sea and cliff that the single row of cottages takes up all the available space and leaves no room for a proper road. This also means that the houses are very close to the sea.

'Are we going to eat this morning?'

The sound of John's voice behind them made both girls jump. They had been so enjoying just standing there and staring that they had not heard their brothers stirring.

Jandy scuttled guiltily into the kitchen and hastily began her breakfast preparations.

'How do you all want your eggs?' she called. 'Boiled or scrambled?'

'Which is quicker?' demanded John.

'Scrambled, I think.'

'Then we'll all have them scrambled,' said her brother in a voice that brooked no argument.

Having checked that (to her great relief) Jandy did not need her help, Shona set off with Hamish for his much-delayed walk now, promising to be 'only a minute'. Ten minutes later she had still not returned and as her egg was congealing on her plate, Jandy went out to look for her. She found her young sister just a little way up the village, standing gazing with rapt attention at something apparently fixed to the wall of the village Hall.

'What was so interesting up there?' asked Jandy curiously as her sister came running up at last in answer to her call. The Hall was a general purpose building that served the Gowrie for every function under the sun. It was the church on Sundays, the meeting-place for the Old Folks' Club on Tuesdays and for the Women's Institute on Thursdays. It also became a concert hall, a polling-station and the venue for public gatherings as the need arose. To Jandy's knowledge, however, it had never held much interest for Shona.

'Well, have you ever heard of the Gowrie Festival?' demanded her sister. 'There's a notice all about it in the Hall window. There's to be a concert tonight—the Grand Anniversary Concert, it says, with recitations and conjuring tricks and community singing. All are welcome!'

'Any refreshments?' asked John. 'If not, I'm not interested.'

'Yes, it says tea will be served,' said Shona. 'Oh, can we all go. Even Robbie?'

'Well, I suppose it might be good for a laugh,' said John grinning. 'What do you think, Jan?'

Jandy was all for the project but insisted that Robbie must promise to have a rest in the afternoon if he was to be allowed to stay up late.

Robbie nodded vigorously, his mouth being too full for speech. He was willing to promise anything for such a treat.

The children went their various ways for the main part of the day. John idled on the jetty, making a half-hearted attempt at some photography, the little ones played on the beach and Jandy had an enjoyable time catching up on the year's gossip, with some of the village ladies. At two o'clock, she remembered about Robbie and went off to find him.

As she expected, he was down on the shore but he came as soon as he was called, laden with treasures he had found there.

'I must keep this one at least,' he pleaded, when ordered sternly to leave the disreputable collection outside. 'See, it's a stone ball and I can scrape off all these wee white bits and keep it beside my bed at home.'

Jandy relented but only on that one point. The stone certainly was an unusual shape and picking off the barnacles would keep Robbie occupied for hours.

Over tea, John gave them some information about the 'Festival'. He had been asking some of the locals about it.

'They say it's held every year to mark the anniversary of the foundation of the village. We've never heard about it before because we've always been up in summer till now.'

'It must be connected with Alec Johnston, then,' remarked Jandy. 'Oh we can't miss this!'

'Maybe we'll be guests of honour, as descendants of the founder,' suggested John. 'Better dress up, Shona. You'll probably have to be one of the platform party!'

This facetious remark was treated with the derision it deserved but nevertheless the children did feel a certain sense of responsibility towards the success of the concert when they discovered what it was in aid of. They were all ready, scrubbed and changed well before the advertised starting time. Not wanting to be first at the Hall, they settled down to wait in the living-room, keeping a watchful eye on the window for the arrival of the audience, who would all have to pass No. 63.

Soon the first concert-goers came past, at first in twos and threes but then in larger, family groups. It seemed as if the whole population of the surrounding countryside was coming to the Gowrie Festival concert.

19

'We'd better go,' said Shona desperately as the others still lingered. 'We won't get in if we don't hurry!'

Her fears were slightly exaggerated, as it turned out, for the hall was hardly half-full when they reached it. They found good seats for themselves right in the centre of the middle row and settled down to enjoy the evening.

'I would never have thought Mr Spiller could sing anything but hymns,' Jandy whispered to her brother at the end of the first item. This was a 'bothy ballad'—an Aberdeen-shire farm song—rendered in a totally authentic accent by one of the local fishermen. As Jandy had said, he was better known as a leading light in the Sunday Meeting choir but the applause he received for his efforts showed how successful this new role was.

Succeeding turns included conjuring tricks by another old villager, poetry recitations on local subjects by the poet him-self and an action song performed by some Porterfield children whose families had Gowrie connections.

At 8.30 there was an interval during which the promised refreshments appeared.

'I'm glad we didn't have much of a tea,' John said loudly for the benefit of the ladies who were dispensing cakes and sandwiches. 'This is really super!'

Jandy gave him an indignant glare. She knew just how much of a tea he had had and she considered that it had been very much. Still even she found it hard to resist Gowrie home-baking.

The last part of the evening consisted of community singing. The songs were mainly old ones—songs about Bonnie Prince Charlie and the clansmen who had followed him, dating back to the early days of Gowrie. Sheets with the words typed on them were handed out and the Turnbulls found themselves—confirmed pop fans though they were in Edinburgh—joining in lustily with 'Come O'er the Stream

20

Charlie' and 'The Young Chevalier' as if these were among the latest hits.

All too soon the evening came to an end and the closing hymn was announced. This was the usual finale to any social occasion in Gowrie as, like most fisherfolk, the local people were very devout and would not have any frivolity too near the Sabbath.

'That was marvellous,' said Jandy dreamily as they made their way back to the cottage. 'Isn't it lovely to be back!'

'Yes, and to feel that you really belong here,' agreed John. 'Everyone in that hall tonight had some old link with Gowrie. That's what I love about this place.'

Robbie was marching ahead of the others, talking, it seemed, to himself.

'What's that you're saying?' asked Shona curiously as she caught up with him.

'And we shall see their like no more

'Till Gowrie Head touch Gowrie shore,' intoned Robbie, matching his steps to the rhythm of the verse.

'Is that a bit of Mr Lawson's poem?' said Shona. 'Fancy you remembering it!'

'I'm good at remembering things!' cried Robbie indignantly. 'It's just like a song.'

He went on repeating the couplet over and over again until Shona begged him to stop. When this had no effect, she appealed to Jandy for help.

'That's enough, Rob,' she said, in her most authoritative big-sister voice. 'You're just spoiling a good poem. I wonder what it means, anyway?'

'I suppose it just means that exciting times like that will never happen again for Gowrie Head will never touch the shore.'

'I jolly well hope it won't!' said Jandy feelingly. Gowrie Head was the massive headland between Gowrie and Porterfield

21

and the thought of seeing it move even an inch was enough to scare anyone.

There was no dawdling on the way to bed tonight. Less than an hour after leaving the concert, all four Turnbulls were abed and No. 63 was in darkness.

The Storm

A loud crash brought John simultaneously awake and bolt upright in bed. Quick as his immediate reaction had been, however, it took quite a time for him to decide just what had happened.

Had Robbie fallen out of bed? No, a quick glance over to the corner reassured him on that point. The Dormouse was as sound asleep and safely cocooned as ever. Only Tibby's sleepy head poking enquiringly over the hump of her bed-mate showed that she too had been disturbed by something.

John turned over other possibilities in his mind. He had better check up on the girls, for one thing. Reluctantly, for he was very comfortable as he was, he heaved himself out of bed and padded over to the adjoining room. He was met in the doorway by the two excited girls.

'What happened?' they chorused. 'Did you drop something?'

'Oh, have a heart!' said John. 'I'm not in the habit of taking ton-weights to bed with me. I think it must have been something outside.'

Just then the room was lit up by a single lurid flash and as the explanation of the noise dawned on them all, the storm struck.

22

The children stood at the sky-light window gazing out, scarcely able to credit the scene. They had gone to bed on a clear, beautifully calm night and now it was like another world out there.

Certainly the sea at that moment bore no resemblance to the friendly water they had bathed and boated in so often.

'Just look at those waves!' squealed Shona. 'I've never seen such monster ones before!'

Tall breakers with angry white crests were rolling in to shore, crashing on the rocks and then retreating menacingly, to pile up offshore again ready for another onslaught. Such was the force of the waves that their spray was actually striking the upstairs window where the children stood.

The crash of the waves, the howling of the wind which had suddenly sprung up and the intermittent crack of the thunder all combined with the rattling of every door and window frame in the house to produce a truly awesome sound effect and to round off the weirdness there was the eerie light of the moon shining over all and imparting an un-earthly air to the scene.

At first the girls squealed afresh at each spectacular wave as it dashed itself against the rocks and even more at each vivid flash of lightning but the display went on too long for them to be able to keep it up. They had fallen silent and were watching in fascination the show going on outside their window and Jandy was just beginning to think that she ought to go and check that Robbie was all right when events took a new and more frightening turn. There was one cataclysmic gust of wind which shook the very cottage—two-foot thick walls and all—and as a sort of exclamation mark after it came a long, drawn-out rumble.

Jandy and John looked at one another. (Shona apparently did not notice this latest development.) Then John came to a quick decision.

'Shona, you'll catch your death of cold if you stand here much longer. Why don't you take this wretched hound into our room and keep Robbie company? You can get into my bed and keep warm while we go downstairs and make something hot to drink.'

Though offended at the reference to the 'wretched hound', Shona was only too glad to accept this suggestion. She *had* been feeling a bit chilly and the storm was beginning to pall.

'Come on, Hamish,' she said. 'Come and see Robbie. He's your friend.'

Once downstairs, John seized Jandy's arm.

'Well,' he said, 'did you think the same as I did? What did that last noise remind you of?'

'It was like that time up Ben Lawers when someone sent a stone spinning downhill and then a big chunk of the hillside went after it,' answered Jandy slowly.

'Exactly—a landslide,' said John. 'The point is: where was it? If it was on the hill behind the house here, we could be in dead trouble.'

Jandy felt fear clutching at her heart but tried not to show her brother how terrified she felt. She paused to control her voice before replying.

'What should we do, do you think?' she asked.

'I'll have to try and find out exactly what happened,' said John. 'Then we can decide what to do. We may have to get out of here and move along the village—to the shop, maybe. Or it might actually be safer to stay where we are.'

Jandy nodded, striving all the time not to tremble too obviously.

'Are you game,' continued her brother, 'to stay behind in the house on your own while I'm out? You can make some hot chocolate—the kids will like that—and we'll all have some when I get back.'

24

Jandy could keep up the brave front no longer.

'Oh, John, you'll have to be careful,' she cried. 'That wind will blow you off your feet—and the water's coming right up over the bankie. You'll have to keep in close to the houses—and put on all the clothes you have!'

'Sure thing,' said John. 'I'm no hero but it would be plain daft just to sit here and wait for disaster without doing anything about it.'

As they spoke they had begun to busy themselves about their various tasks. There was a moment of dismay when John tried to switch on the light and found that the electricity supply was apparently one casualty of the storm but there was still enough fitful light from outside to allow them to move around, mainly because the room was so familiar to them.

'Probably better without electricity in a thunderstorm anyway,' said John, fumbling for his shoes. 'Thank goodness the gas works by pilot. It always gives some light.'

That was a blessing, thought Jandy. Then she said aloud,

'I think there are some candles in the cupboard. Will you help me to look before you go?'

They were in luck. On the top shelf of the food cupboard was a white cardboard shoe-box which on investigation by the light of the gas ring proved to contain about a dozen fat, white candles. Jandy took out a couple and lit them both at the gas flame.

Meanwhile John fetched two saucers and, letting some grease drip from the candles on to each, formed little pools of melted wax with which he could fix the candles upright.

'That's much better,' said Jandy with satisfaction. 'Now it's not nearly so gloomy.'

And indeed her spirits were beginning to lift a little now that she was actually doing something.

'Well,' said John. 'I'll be off. Now don't worry. I'm not

25

going to do anything stupid but don't expect me back too soon. I'll have to take my time.'

Saying this, he unlocked the door and turned the handle. Immediately pandemonium broke out. An icy blast of wind shot into the room, blowing out the candles and sending various small objects spinning across the floor. Temporarily winded as the force of the door struck his chest, John could not move for a few minutes but eventually he recovered and then he battled his way outside in the face of the storm and with a superhuman effort pulled the door closed behind him.

Poor Jandy's high spirits evaporated in a moment as she saw what had happened and she stood still for a few minutes after the door had closed behind her brother, struggling hard not to cry. She was worried about so many things: about John being out there in that foul weather, about the terrible weight of responsibility for the two little ones and the two pets upstairs and, on top of that now, about the depressing prospect of having to set the kitchen to rights after the incursion of the wind. Then she pulled herself together.

'No,' she told herself severely. 'Crying is a luxury you cannot afford. Work! That's how to forget your troubles.' And quite without her bidding, the words of a hymn they had learnt that year at school came into her head—'Work, for the Night is coming.'

It was a real, old Victorian hymn and Jandy had not liked it specially at the time but now it provided the perfect accompaniment to her labours and with its aid she re-lit the candles, tidied up the room and made four mugs of steaming hot chocolate ready on the table, almost without noticing it. Next, she rummaged among the biscuit tins and found some digestive and some chocolate biscuits. These she put on a plate. Then she paused.

'Should I take them up to the wee ones?' she wondered.

'Or would it be better to bring them down here?'

Now that the momentum of her activity had been broken, she was plunged once more into indecision. She would have welcomed John's advice on this point and was afraid of failing him by deciding the wrong way. Normally she would not have spent two seconds worrying about anything so trivial but tonight nothing was normal. When John was taking such risks it was particularly important that she should back him up at home. She had just decided that she would at least go upstairs to check that Shona and Robbie were all right when a pounding at the door announced the return of John. She hurried over to open up for him.

'Quick, let me in!' cried her brother. 'I'm perished!'

This time she was prepared for the violence of the weather and she held the door steady with one foot while she helped to pull John in from the grasp of the wind which seemed reluctant to let him go and indeed gave every appearance of wanting to suck her out too. When John was safely inside the room she threw her weight against the door until it was securely locked once more. She stayed like that, facing her brother, as she braced herself to hear what he had to tell.

John's Story

'It's even worse out there than we thought,' John told her when he had recovered his breath sufficiently to speak at all.

He had, it seemed, almost been blown off his feet as soon as he left the shelter of the house and had stood literally clutching the door-post as an anchor for a few minutes before attempting to venture farther into the open.

27

'I couldn't see anything at first,' he said, 'for the rain was absolutely lashing down into my face and I couldn't even keep my eyes open. Then I pulled my anorak hood forward to give my face at least a bit of shelter and it wasn't so bad after that.'

He paused to pull off his wet jacket and kicked off his shoes at the same time. Jandy ran to fetch his slippers which she had thoughtfully heated at the fire.

'Your shoes are soaking!' she cried in horror as she picked them up. 'You'd better have a basin of hot water to warm up your feet. You'll catch your death of cold.'

'No fear,' answered her brother. 'If you'll just get me a towel, I'll give them a good rub and that'll bring the circulation back. Tell you what I would like though—a good hot drink.'

'It's ready,' Jandy said, handing him a towel, 'but tell me what you discovered outside before I go up for the others.'

'Well,' continued John, vigorously towelling his cold feet, 'I finally managed to get along the "bankie" as far as McFarlane's corner and, wow, was the wind strong! You've never imagined anything like it. The only thing that saved me was the fact that it was blowing in towards the shore. Otherwise I'd have been sent spinning into the sea. As it was, I was thrown against McFarlane's door and gave my head one terrific thump.'

'Let's see,' said Jandy. 'Is it bleeding?'

John shook his head, impatient of the interruption.

'Luckily my anorak hood's well padded. Well anyway, that was how it went all the way along. I lost count of how many times I fell and how many bumps and bruises I collected. It wouldn't have been so bad if it had been only dark or windy or wet but all three things together were pretty awful I can tell you.'

At this point Jandy could hardly restrain herself from

bursting out, 'But what did you find out?' It was not that she was unsympathetic to John's troubles but after all he was home and dry again now and still she did not know whether or not they were all going to have to go out into the storm. However she knew better than to keep pestering her brother with questions. If she did, he was quite likely to prolong her agony for sheer devilment. So she said nothing but merely made suitably sympathetic noises.

'Just as I was thinking I would never get there,' John went on, 'I found myself at the part where the path slopes down to the burn. I was really making for the shop, you see, for that seemed the surest place to get news and I was telling myself that it wouldn't be long now when I realized that there were people across on the other bank. I could see lights moving about and hear the sound of men shouting.

'I don't know what made me go down the slope to the bridge specially carefully—you know how you can hardly help running at that part—maybe it was because I didn't want to risk landing on my nose again. Anyhow I didn't run and it was just as well for I suddenly realized that there was no bridge there any more. If I'd gone down full tilt as usual, I'd have ended up in the water and been swept out to sea in no time.'

Jandy gasped, all her impatience at John's story forgotten. She felt again the sour taste of fear in her mouth that was becoming such a feature of this dreadful night and her throat had gone suddenly dry. For a moment no words came when she tried to speak. Then she ventured,

'Does that mean we're cut off?'

'Not only that. We're marooned on our own at this end of the village. Mrs Wood's not in her house. She must have stayed the night up at the farm.'

'Did—did you manage to speak to anyone at the burn?' asked Jandy.

29

'Not at first. I shouted two or three times but I might as well have saved my breath. I couldn't even hear myself! Then I tried to throw a handful of pebbles but they blew right back into my face. Just as I was losing hope altogether, I thought of flashing my torch—I had been trying to save the battery in case of a real emergency—and thank goodness someone noticed me at last. I think it was Mr Wood from the shop but I couldn't even be sure of that and although he called over to me, I could scarcely make out a word.''

Jandy was unable to repress a shudder at the picture John's story conjured up. She was living every moment over again with him and she could just imagine the scene as he stood on the unfenced bank of the burn, trying to keep his footing in that terrible gale and straining at the same time to hear what might be vital news from the other side.

'I didn't want to stay out there too long because of the danger,' continued her brother, 'but I did gather that there's been a landslide at Gowrie Head—that must have been the sound we heard—and that some of the houses at that end have been damaged quite badly.'

Relief flooded over Jandy. Bad though the news was, it sounded fairly hopeful for them.

'So is it safe enough behind us here?' she asked. 'If that end is getting the worst of the storm, we should be OK, shouldn't we?'

John nodded.

'I should think so,' he replied. 'We're more sheltered here and there'd be no point in moving down to the other end. To tell the truth, I doubt if Robbie for one could keep his feet in that gale, anyway.'

'Oh I'm glad we're not having to go,' breathed Jandy. 'I was dreading having to go out there.' She stood up with new confidence. 'Well, now that's fixed we may as well have our chocolate. I'll go and fetch the others. It's cosier down here.'

John heard these words with something like astonishment. You never could tell with girls, he reflected. The thought of being stuck away here on their own didn't seem to bother her as long as she didn't have to go out into the storm and she was very confident that their house was going to be safe. Then he shrugged his shoulders in resignation. After all, it would be worse if she were nervous and it would not do the youngsters any good either. This way, she could at least concentrate on her cooking and that was the main thing!

Visitors in the Night

Jandy practically flew up the narrow stair-case to the bedrooms, so light-hearted did she feel. The thought of having to drag the children, not to mention the two pets, out into that evil weather had filled her whole being with dread. Now that there was no need to move, she felt a sense of release coupled with a readiness to face anything new that might arise.

'Come on, you lot!' she called cheerfully as she entered the bedroom. 'We're going to have a midnight feast downstairs. Bring your quilts with you and don't forget to put on your slippers!'

As she spoke, she lifted Tibby from Robbie's bed and gave Hamish an encouraging nudge on the rump.

'You too, old man,' she said. 'There's a snack for dogs as well.'

Shona sprang up willingly to follow her sister. Robbie's idea of entertainment was to relate a non-stop series of jokes and since he laughed so much as he was telling them and frequently missed the point in his excitement besides, the listener tended to become slightly bored. In Shona's case, this was aggravated by the fact that many of the jokes had been hers in the beginning. So a change of scene and company was a welcome prospect.

Seeing his audience desert him so suddenly, Robbie reluctantly rolled out of his quilt and, thrusting his feet into his slippers, came shuffling on behind the others.

They reached the living-room to find John already started on his hot chocolate, having also made deep inroads into the plate of biscuits.

'Hey Jandy,' he greeted his sister, 'how about finding something more filling than this? I'll never last out till breakfast on biscuits alone.'

'I suppose I could open the tin of hamburgers,' she replied doubtfully, 'but that was really meant for dinner tomorrow.'

'Right,' said John decisively. 'A vote's called for. Hands up those who want their hamburgers now.'

There was no need for a count as the vote was unanimous. So Jandy went over to the cupboard to start work. Her mood of cheerfulness still persisted and she hummed as she piled up rolls, butter and onions in readiness on the working surface. Then she carefully opened the giant-sized tin of hamburgers (Contents: 24) at the wall can-opener. The light was rather dim for an operation of this sort and she knew from past experience how easy it was to cut a finger on the sharp edge of the lid. So she took no chances and concentrated hard on her task.

She had just accomplished this and had moved on to light the gas in order to start cooking when another strange crashing sound from outside stopped her in her tracks. She paused to listen. Really, her first chance to do the family cooking was not being given ideal conditions.

The other three, who had been whiling away the hungry

32

minutes with Robbie's favourite game of I-Spy (not an easy matter in the gloom) paused too. There was so much general din outside that it was difficult to distinguish any of the component sounds.

'I never knew before that the weather could be so noisy,' exclaimed Jandy. 'I've always liked lying in bed listening to the sound of the wind until now.'

'That wasn't just the wind a minute ago,' said John. 'It seemed to come from the shore—as if something was being dashed against the rocks.'

'Listen!' hissed Shona. 'I hear voices.'

'Maybe a party has come to rescue us,' put in Jandy, not altogether pleased at the idea. 'I wonder who it will be?'

Shona meanwhile had darted over to the window to peer out and now she drew back with a yelp of alarm. John, just behind her, was barely in time to see a white blur, that might have been a face, withdraw quickly from the other side of the glass and he had a definite impression of a figure dodging aside.

'It's a ghost!' quavered Shona, clinging to her brother's arm in terror. 'A ghostly white head with burning eyes!'

'Rubbish!' said John firmly, with more assurance in fact than he really felt. 'I saw someone moving away but there were no burning eyes. Whoever it is, is human all right for we all heard the voices—still, they can't be locals or they wouldn't act in that shifty way. They'd come straight to the door.'

He bent over the wide sill towards the window again, straining to see out through the torrents of rain streaming down the panes.

'Here!' he cried suddenly. 'Quick, Jandy! I think there's a boat down there on the shore. Maybe someone's been shipwrecked.'

Jandy joined him at the window, her heart beating faster

each time a gust of wind blew for the violence of the gale was actually forcing the window-frame to bulge and bend inwards and she did not feel at all safe standing so near to it. However she was getting better at putting on at least a show of courage and no-one guessed what an effort it cost her to remain there feigning interest in what was going on outside.

Yes, there was just enough light from the moon when it was not obscured by the scudding storm-clouds for her to discern that there was something unusual down there on the foreshore. It was not one of the familiar rock shapes and the only other likely object in such a position was a boat but the rain on the window-glass kept coming between her and the view.

'It does look like a boat,' she said slowly, thinking how awful it would be if it should prove to be one of the local fishing fleet. 'What should we do about it? Will we go and see if there's anything we can do to help?' She spoke without much conviction for to tell the truth she did not really see what help they could give. There was no question, for instance, of rescuing anyone from the sea in its present turbulent state.

Before John had a chance to answer however, the problem resolved itself. In the wake of an unusually noisy surge of weather came an echoing roll as someone hammered at the cottage door.

For a moment all of the children remained motionless, staring at one another and too paralysed by shock or fear to move. John was the first to pull himself together.

'You get over there out of the way with the wee ones,' he whispered to Jandy at last, 'but move the candles first. This is one time when we certainly don't want to be left in darkness. I'll go to the door.'

Obediently, although inwardly she was questioning the need to answer the door at all, Jandy shifted the candles to a more sheltered position and then she joined Shona and Robbie on the big settee where they were cosily muffled up in their quilts with the two pets in attendance. That is to say, Tibby was actually on the settee, curled up beside Robbie and Hamish was sleeping peacefully underneath. However, as John engaged once more in the now-routine struggle with the storm-battered door, a black shape suddenly streaked out from the corner and joined his master in a convincing watch-dog pose at the door.

Again the door was blown violently open as John unlocked it but this time the effect of the weather was nothing compared with the effect of the man who stood on the threshold. John was tall for a fourteen-year-old but beside the visitor he appeared undersized to say the least.

At first he was so taken aback by the sheer girth of the stranger that, unmindful of good manners or even of his personal comfort, he could only gape wordlessly. Because of the poor light, all he got was an impression of size but that was enough to leave him speechless, all the while holding the door open to the elements in a helpless way. Then the man spoke.

'Mile mathanasan gun robh mi a'cur dragh oirbh air oidhche mar seo, ach . . .'

('A thousand pardons for disturbing you on such a night as this, but . . .')

He broke off without finishing the sentence as John shook his head uncomprehendingly. John swallowed hard. This was something he had no experience of and he was not sure how to deal with it.

'I-I'm sorry,' he stammered, 'but could you say that in English?'

The stranger raised an apologetic hand.

'Fool that I am,' he said. 'Of course the people of the sea-coast have not the Gaelic. My humble apologies, sir.

35

'A company of us have been stranded here on your shore by this accursed gale and we know not where we have landed. We must be in Banff for the going out of the tide tomorrow. Is that place far distant from here?'

All the while as he spoke, the wind and rain kept up their relentless attack on the house and John, standing in the doorway and wrestling to keep the door open while maintaining the civilities as head of the house, finally realized that he had no choice but to invite the stranger into the house. Though formidable in appearance, the man seemed polite enough, whatever else he might prove to be.

'Will you come in,' said John, standing aside a little. 'Please don't frighten my sisters and little brother though. We weren't expecting visitors at this time of night.'

The stranger bowed his head in courteous acknowledgement of these words and stepped past him into the room.

Making Friends

For a moment it seemed to the children as if the newcomer filled the room. There was an awkward pause until Jandy recollected her duty and ventured over shyly to show him to the biggest easy chair. John was too busy waging the familiar battle with the door to play the part of host. He was in the act of giving the door a final push to close it when he became aware of the presence of more figures hovering uncertainly just beyond the threshold. Obviously they were part of the stranger's company and since they made no attempt to force their way in to join their friend, John quickly decided that they were to be trusted.

'Your friends had better come in too,' he said, turning to the first man, 'but I don't suppose they would understand me. Will you speak to them?'

The big man addressed a few words to those outside and next moment three more men trooped in. At last John managed to get the door fastened.

Now the room really was full. Despite Jandy's precautions one of the candles had been blown out by the draught but the flame of the other still glowed strongly and this, along with the flickering firelight, provided some illumination. The dimness of the room was no great hardship as it allowed the two groups to eye one another surreptitiously without appearing to do so. This they did in silence for a few minutes.

There was plenty in the appearance of their visitors to hold the children's interest for it was eccentric to say the least. The leader, for the first man obviously held that position, seemed to be in some sort of uniform and only he had some trace of smartness in his garb. What his uniform was, however, was a mystery and John who considered himself to be something of an authority on such matters was sure that no modern British regiment would own it. Jandy too was examining his outfit.

'I've never seen a kilt like that before,' she thought. 'It doesn't even have proper pleats. I wonder if he made it himself!'

Sure enough the garment in question was a far cry from the smart kilt of the trendy Highlander to be seen at clan gatherings and similar meetings. It seemed to consist of one single long piece of cloth which went round its wearer's waist in a number of loose folds and ended up over his shoulder where it was fastened to his jacket by a large, ornate clasp. When he had first appeared in the doorway, the big man had been wearing a tammy of sorts with what looked like a white rosette pinned in front of it. This he had pulled from his head when he entered the cottage and he was now clutching it in his hand.

His three companions were much more ragged and unkempt. So tattered were their clothes that it would have been difficult to identify what they wore. The most noticeable difference between them and their leader however was in the matter of footgear. Only the big man had shoes. Of the others, two had their feet bound up in rags while the third man was barefoot.

'They must have lost their shoes in the water when their boat struck the rocks,' Jandy decided. 'But how did their clothes get so ragged? They look as if they have been living rough for ages, poor things.'

John's opinion of their visitors was less charitable.

'They can't be fishermen,' he told himself, 'for they're not wearing oilskins or boots; and no-one in their senses would be out for pleasure on a night like this. So they must be poachers, out to raid the lobster-pots or the salmon nets.'

As the Turnbulls took in these details, they were aware of being equally closely scrutinized and for a space there was an uncomfortable silence. Then John felt that he had to take the initiative.

'My name's John Turnbull,' he said, 'and these are my sisters, Jandy and Shona. This is Robbie. We've been cut off here by the storm—the bridge that links us with the village is down—but if we can give you any help, you're welcome to it.'

'We are indeed grateful to you,' said the first man, who was apparently the only one with any command of English. 'It is no simple thing to take pity on strangers on such a night as this and in these troubled times. May your kindness earn you the reward you deserve.'

This courteous speech aroused Jandy's hospitable instincts and encouraged her to make her own contribution to the general goodwill.

'I expect you're all cold and hungry,' she said. 'We were just going to have something to eat and there's plenty to share—if you like hamburgers, that is?'

'Anything you offer us will be welcome indeed,' replied the stranger, 'for we have had to eat some strange fare in these past months. But we do not wish to take the bread from the mouths of these little ones and must not impose on your kindness.'

Jandy could not understand much of this flowery speech, partly because of the speaker's strong Highland accent, but she took it to be a polite way of accepting the offer of food. This suited her plans and she thankfully seized the excuse of continuing with her preparations which had been interrupted by the arrival of the visitors. It was while she was thus occupied that Hamish decided to make friends with the big man and this broke the ice more effectively than anything else.

'Ah, it's the true Gael you have there,' said the big man, holding the candle in his hand in order to have a better look at the Scottie. 'A fine beast, a fine beast—bred by the chieftains of the West for the hunting and loyal to the core.'

Hamish rubbed his head against the stranger's leg in an unusual display of friendship and Shona, encouraged by this praise of her favourite, gradually edged closer to the visitors. Soon Robbie, with Tibby in his arms, was over making friends too.

Suddenly Shona let out a little squeal of dismay.

'You've been hurt,' she cried, staring in horror at the man nearest her. 'There's blood all down your face!'

This was a chance that Shona was not going to miss. Her great ambition was to become a nurse and not, as her cynical family said, simply because of the attractive uniform. She took advantage of every opportunity that came her way to practise her skills and always attended to Robbie's cuts and bruises. So the drill on this occasion was quite familiar to her.

There was a first-aid box under the sink and Shona poked around in the dark until she found this. Then, armed with a bowl of warm water to which she had added some disinfectant, she advanced on her patient.

He was a young man with a shock of untidy, fair hair and, unlike the others, was clean-shaven. His clothes were more ragged than any of the others', consisting of an untidy kilt and a jacket so worn that it seemed to consist of more holes than material.

At first Shona was fully occupied in cleaning up the cut head. It was no easy task in the dim light provided by the candles and she was conscious every time she touched a tender spot for the wounded man flinched with pain although he uttered no sound of complaint. It was obviously a very bad gash and as she applied a bandage to the wound after it was cleaned, she wondered what had caused it. This and her natural instinct for chat made her open a conversation.

'You haven't told us your names yet, you know,' she remarked. 'We don't even know where you've come from or how you got your sore head.'

No-one answered for a moment. John held his breath, waiting to hear the reply. He had been pondering how to find out that very information without asking outright. Trust Shona to take the direct approach!

Then the big man, as usual, acted as spokesman.

'Well now,' he said slowly, 'perhaps the less you know of these matters the better it will be for your own safety. People such as we only bring trouble on the like of you.'

John leaned forward in excitement. This seemed to confirm his own suspicions. Honest men would not bring trouble on anyone and he was about to pursue the matter when Shona persisted,

'But can't you just tell us your names? That couldn't get anyone into bother.'

The big man had a quick exchange of Gaelic with his comrades, obviously to ask their advice. Then he said,

'Forgive my discourtesy in speaking my own tongue but my companions know little English. We have learnt to think well before speaking in recent times,' he went on, turning to Shona, 'but it would be a poor return for your kindness to us were we to refuse your request. My companions are Domhnull here,' he indicated the man next to him, 'and Iain Ban of the broken head; yon is Cailean and among the Lowlanders, I am most often called Roy. More than that it would be no kindness to tell you.'

'You said you might bring trouble to us,' said John, at last having a chance to speak. 'Are you escaped convicts or something—or fugitives from justice, maybe? Is that why you were out in a boat on a night like this?'

Again Big Roy paused to think before answering.

'We're fugitives, yes,' he replied at last, 'but not from any justice that we recognize. We have been fugitives in our own land ever since Drummossie, hunted like beasts on moor and mountain until—'

He broke off suddenly, as if realizing that his tongue had been running on too freely and finished,

'—but you had better not know too much about that lest you fall into the hands of the Redcoats and are forced to tell.'

John felt as if his head was spinning—Drummossie? Redcoats? What was he talking about? And what sort of men had he brought into the house?

As his mind was busily working, trying to make sense of these fragments of information, the mournful soughing of the wind and the battering of the rain against the window kept going on in the background, adding to the general unreality of the night. And yet, John had to admit to

41

himself, in some ways everything was so ordinary. Shona, Robbie and most of all, Hamish appeared to have made themselves quite at home with their visitors and Jandy seemed too absorbed in her cooking to pay much attention to anything else.

'Am I imagining things?' thought John, 'or is everything really as queer as it seems to me?'

He had been conscious all the time of something in Roy's words niggling at the back of his mind but what it was he just could not recollect, try as he might. The name 'Drummossie', he thought, meant something to him but he could not place it. As he was puzzling over it, however, Jandy announced that the food was ready and John remembered that he was hungry.

His sister had thoroughly enjoyed this chance to exercise her skills and while the others had been talking she had been happily frying onions and hamburgers and buttering rolls which she then piled with the filling. This absorbing work had left her more or less oblivious to the conversation going on around her. Now she proudly passed a laden plateful to each of the visitors.

'There's only hot chocolate to drink, I'm afraid,' she apologized, 'for we've run out of tea-bags. Will that do?'

Everyone was too busily engaged in eating to answer this but Jandy took the fact that no-one refused her offer to mean that all were accepting it. Judging from the way the men seized on the rolls and delved into them, they must all have been almost starving; all, that is, except their leader.

He very noticeably did not eat his food immediately. Instead, he was sniffing at it and examining it as well as he could in the poor light. This was so much at odds with his former good manners that Jandy could not help watching him, wondering anxiously what was wrong with her cooking.

'What is this that you are giving us?' demanded big Roy at

last, and his tone was far from friendly. 'White bread and fresh meat—and offering us chocolate to drink! Why, such luxuries are known only to the fine ladies at the French court—or so I've heard tell. What manner of house is this that you can offer such dainties to poor men? Are you in the employ of the English?'

'English?' echoed John indignantly, catching on to the only part of this speech that seemed to make sense. 'Indeed we're not! We're from Edinburgh and what we're eating is just what we have at home, and the same as everyone else eats.'

'Ah, Dunedin is it?' replied the other, somehow mollified by this explanation. 'Yes, I have heard that even the common people live high there but this I would never have believed. It is not what they gave us last August when we were there—but then, that was another matter.'

He broke off to address some words in Gaelic to the other men again and after that the atmosphere grew more relaxed. Everyone was too busy eating to talk until, that is, Jandy came round with the hot drinks.

She was offering a cup of chocolate to one of the hitherto silent men when, to her surprise, instead of accepting it he plucked at her sleeve and whispered urgently to her.

'You would not be having a taste of the "uisge beath" [whisky] now, would you? Or even a drop of claret?'

His sidelong glance towards the big man all the while and his nervous manner as he made this request were explained the next minute. Roy's wrath was something to behold. He rounded on his luckless companion with a roar.

'Black, burning shame on you Domhnull Dubh,' he cried, 'to be asking such a thing of your hosts. Is this the conduct of a MacIan? The black sorrow be upon you for this affront on our clan.'

The unfortunate Domhnull sank back into his seat,

crushed by this rebuke, and took the proffered cup without another word. The big man obviously wielded authority in the group, even to the extent of speaking for those who could speak some English.

As if to make up for the rudeness of Domhnull Dubh then, Roy made a particular show of enjoying his chocolate. He raised his mug before drinking and, looking round the group, said, 'Your very good health, sirs and ladies . . .'

'I know what we should say,' John interrupted, forgetting his own good manners in his excitement for he had just dredged up his only word of Gaelic from somewhere at the back of his memory. 'Slainte! That's it, isn't it?'

These well-meaning words had a curious effect. Tension returned among the Highlanders and their leader leaned forward and spoke in low, urgent tones.

'So you do have the Gaelic. Well now, if that be so, I have a better toast than that for you.'

He paused to set down his mug and fumbled for a moment in his pocket. The children's eyes were growing more accustomed to the gloom by this time but, even so, it was hard to tell by the flickering candlelight what exactly he had produced but as they gathered closer to see better they were able to distinguish what looked like a silk handkerchief. This Roy carefully spread out on the table and then gestured to everyone to join him in raising their cups.

'I give you: the King over the Water!' he said solemnly, holding his mug, as he spoke, over the spread-out hand-kerchief.

'The King over the Water,' they all repeated obediently, although the words had no meaning for them. Even Robbie was so impressed by the atmosphere that he got it right.

When the electric moment had passed and the others were all seated again he remained at the table with Shona, examining the handkerchief.

44

'Who is the lady in the picture?' he asked, peering at the silk square. 'And why did you lay your hanky out like that?'

'It's not a lady, silly,' hissed Shona. 'It's an old-fashioned man with long hair. See, he's wearing a soldier's uniform.'

These words supplied the missing connection that John had been searching for. Suddenly all the jigsaw pieces came together in his mind. There was so much that was odd about their visitors—the strange garments, the Gaelic speech and most of all the references to 'Drummossie', 'the King' and 'fugitives'. He was so excited that he hardly dared breathe what was in his mind yet he was fairly sure that he knew the answer to the mystery.

Danger on the Hill

Before John could speak however Robbie again created a diversion. All this time he had been clutching his round stone, picking surreptitiously at the barnacles and yet still somehow managing to eat his roll. The crunch came when he tried to pick up his mug of chocolate too. Then something had to go and that something was the stone. It fell to the floor with a resounding clatter which made everyone jump.

The wounded man, Iain Ban, bent to retrieve it but when he picked it up and saw by the light of the candle what was in his hand it had a strange effect on him. Excitedly he turned to his friends and made some remark in Gaelic and for a few minutes a lively discussion ensued among them. Then their leader spoke.

'Where did you get this, a Laochain?' he asked, turning to

45

Robbie. 'It's a strange thing for a young lad in these parts to have a lead shot in his possession.'

'It's my stone ball,' protested Robbie. 'I found it on the beach this afternoon and I'm cleaning it up to keep it.'

'A stone ball is it?' said Roy. 'Aye, but it's a ball that has done its bit for our cause.'

John could keep silence on what was in his mind no longer.

'I think I know who you are!' he cried. 'You're Jacobites and you've been fighting at Culloden. You said something about having to be in Banff in time for the tide going out tomorrow—is that because you're meaning to sail with the tide? Maybe you're going to escape for you're fugitives from the soldiers of the Duke of Cumberland, I think. Am I right?'

In his excitement, he had risen without really knowing it and was now standing beside Big Roy who had also got to his feet. He was staring down at John.

'Hush, young sir,' he whispered hoarsely. 'Do you not know the danger of speaking openly about such matters? Yes, you are in the right as to who we are and whither we are bound but there are some things that are better kept unsaid.' He seized John's arm and made a sign to enjoin silence as he sat down again and then he went on in a low voice.

'The Butcher's men were at our heels when we put to sea tonight and even now they may still be after us. They do not give up easily and they have many old scores to settle with the MacIans. Their spies are everywhere and some of them may have seen the boat driven ashore here.'

'Surely not in weather like this,' objected John. 'You can hardly see the boat from this house and you certainly couldn't see it from any distance because of the darkness and the storm.'

'I tell you, their spies are everywhere,' repeated the other. 'Who knows but that they might be lurking in the next house to this! Or the people there may be in the Redcoats' pay.'

The very thought of friendly Mrs Wood being a spy in anyone's service would have amused John at any other time but his companion was too serious for his words to be treated lightly.

This conversation was quite above the heads of the younger Turnbulls although they had enough idea of its importance to remain silent. Jandy on the other hand had listened in astonishment as the identity of their visitors was disclosed. She had been worried that they might be criminals of some sort although they seemed too gentlemanly for that to be so but to discover that they were actually men from another century was scarcely less worrying. It was really too fantastic to contemplate and partly to escape from the confusion of her thoughts she now spoke.

'We're only five miles from Banff here,' she contributed, 'but it's a terrible night for walking and since we're cut off from the rest of the village by the storm your only way out would be over the hill behind the houses.'

'But at least,' added John, 'we're safe from the Redcoats too for nobody can get in or out of the village because of the landslide.'

As if on cue, as he finished speaking came a sound which momentarily silenced everyone in the room. Even in the midst of the raging of the storm it was clearly heard for this sound was at the back of the house where the weather was much less violent. It was the unmistakable sound of a stone or similar hard object striking the back wall of the house and when it was followed soon after by a succession of like sounds the explanation was obvious. Jandy grabbed her brother's arm and her voice trembled as she whispered,

'It's the hill, John. It's coming down on the house after all. What are we going to do?'

'I'm not so sure,' he replied quietly. 'I don't think a landslip would begin like that—at least not one caused by

47

the weather. Seems to be more as if there's something moving out there and that's what has disturbed the stones.'

Big Roy was equally interested in the strange noises and now he uttered a low 'Hush now!' and raised a hand in warning. Everyone sat silent, straining to hear any repetition of the sounds. A low rumbling in the back of Hamish's throat was all that disturbed the quiet in the room as he crouched with his ears pricked attentively, staring at the back wall.

This lasted for a moment. Then, just as the tension was easing, there was another bump on the back of the house, followed by a rattle of lesser noises.

The uncertainty was too much for Jandy and as so often happens at such times, desperation made her brain work more quickly than usual.

'The bathroom window!' she said suddenly, more loudly than she intended. Then she went on in a whisper, 'We may be able to see something from there.'

This was an inspiration. The bathroom, which had been converted from a net store in the original cottage, was the only part of the house which gave a view of the hillside at the back. Because it was something of an afterthought and did not conform with the plan of the rest of the cottage which of course faced the sea, it was easy to forget about this window.

John nodded in response to his sister's words and went over to Big Roy.

'Come with me,' he whispered, 'and I'll show you where we can go to see what's happening out there.'

It was noticeable, even in the excitement of the moment, how silently the big man moved. The house was strange to him and he had had no chance to see it properly. The candle lit up only its own immediate surroundings. Yet not a sound did the Jacobite make, either in moving or by colliding with objects in his way. Even John who was quite familiar with the room was much noisier.

48

In the bathroom it was pitch-black except for where the window showed as a paler oblong in the rear wall. The two made their way over to this and peered out.

At first John could distinguish nothing in the darkness outside but gradually he was able to discern blacker shapes here and there denoting familiar objects such as the big outcrop of rock where they always draped their towels after bathing in summer-time. Then a sharp intake of breath from his companion made John glance at him and then follow the direction of his gaze, which he guessed from the angle of his faintly-seen profile, higher up the hill.

What with the rain streaming down aslant outside and the moving shadows of bushes tossed in the wind, it was hard to be sure of detail but, yes—way up there on the skyline there was movement and it was not that of branches waving in the wind. There were people up there, several of them and as they moved they were bringing down chunks of earth and stone on to the Turnbulls' house.

The two at the window did not linger once they had established this fact. Without a word to each other, they crept back into the living-room and, again by unspoken agreement, each made for his own group there.

John's mind was in a whirl. He had just—only just— managed to absorb the fact that, somehow or other, they had given shelter to men from two and a half centuries back who had contrived to get mixed up with the present time (and yet appeared unaware of the fact). It had been a bit of a puzzle wondering what to do about them but now there was a much more dangerous development. The Redcoats, for he had no doubt at all in his mind that they were the people on the hill since no local would ever do anything so foolhardy, could easily set off a landslide by dislodging rocks which normally never felt the passage of anything bigger than a rabbit. But could a landslide caused by men of the eighteenth century

49

damage a modern house? There was no means of knowing the answer to this and it was not a risk he wanted to take at all events.

Then there was the further complication which had made them stay before. If they were all to move from the cottage, where would they go? There was not a single occupied house that they could reach and the alternative, of spending the night in the open, was too awful to consider.

He decided to tell the others briefly what he had found out and see their reactions.

'There are definitely people up there on the hill,' he said, 'and if the fools caper about like that in the dark they might easily bring down the whole bank on top of this house.'

'Who are they?' asked Shona. 'Maybe it's Mr Wood with a party of rescuers coming to help us.'

John shook his head decisively.

'No way,' he said. 'Mr Wood would never do a silly thing like that. Besides, he's not fit. No, believe it or not, I think it's the Redcoats.'

A sharp intake of breath from Jandy was the only audible reaction to this and John continued,

'Now, I don't know if they could do us any harm but I don't propose to wait here to find out.'

Gratefully, he realized that Jandy was anticipating his decision for she was already busy bundling an unusually docile Robbie into his outdoor clothes. As they occupied themselves in helping the youngsters and preparing for their own encounter with the elements too, the elder Turnbulls held a hasty, whispered consultation.

'You agree that we should get away from here, then?' asked John.

'Of course, but what does it all mean, John? Are the men on the hill really English Redcoats, I mean, the kind you read about? Do you understand what's happening? I find all this a bit scary.'

'I'm not exactly happy about it myself, to tell the truth,' admitted her brother, 'but we don't want Shona and Robbie to get the wind up. So far, thank goodness, they don't seem to be bothered at all.'

It was true. One of the extraordinary things about this oddest of nights was the calm way in which the two youngsters had accepted every strange happening. Even more surprising, Hamish—not normally the stranger's friend—was positively fawning on the visitors while Tibby, the 'nervous' cat, slept peacefully through everything.

'What about them?' went on Jandy, nodding over to the little group of Highlanders. 'How are we to get them away to safety?'

'That's another problem,' agreed John. 'Once we're out of here and have found some kind of shelter, we can think about it but at the moment, they will be as keen to get away from the Redcoats as we are—though for different reasons, maybe.'

As they were completing their preparations, the Jacobite leader came over to them.

'You are leaving too, then?' he said quietly. 'I think it is a wise thing to do. These murderous cut-throats have no mercy on the young and the weak—aye, and I'm the man who has reason to know that . . .'

He might have gone on to explain his words but at that moment another fall of rocks against the house recalled the danger of their situation.

'Now then,' whispered Big Roy urgently, 'do you tell us the best way to go. If we can but win up to the open ground above the town, we shall soon elude the clumsy Sassenachs and then we'll be off to Banff and away on the morning tide before they know they've lost us.'

John thought quickly. There was only one sensible direction to go from the cottage door and that was towards the main part of the village. The other way would only take them hard up against the quite impassable bulk of Carron Head and would leave the fugitives at the mercy of their pursuers. The trouble was that, tonight, with the bridge down they would not be much better off going in the other direction, unless . . . John decided swiftly.

'Go to the left as you leave the house,' he instructed. 'Keep straight on and stay as close in to the houses as you can for the road's very uneven and dangerous at the shore edge. I'll hurry on ahead and look for a place for us to hide until we're sure it's safe for us to try for the hill.'

He was thinking as he spoke of all the dark closes between the cottages at the west end of the village where most of the houses were end-on to the sea. Surely he would be able to find a secure and sheltered corner somewhere among them.

Captives!

It was at this point that Robbie held up proceedings slightly by trying to insert an unwilling cat into her travelling basket, a useless exercise as it turned out.

'But you'll have to go in,' he was protesting. 'You know how you hate the rain!'

'Thoir dhomh am piseag!'* came a voice from the rear and Iain Ban thrust himself forward and, seizing the struggling animal, stowed her inside his plaid in seconds till only her bright eyes, wide open in surprise, showed above the folds.

Now Big Roy stepped noiselessly as usual over to the door and, just as silently, drew it open. A quick glance to each side

*Give me the little cat.

and a brief pause to listen were enough to satisfy him and then he whispered, 'Come!'

Cautiously they filed out. John took the lead but was closely followed by two of the younger Jacobites. Next came Shona with a strangely docile Hamish at her heels. Jandy, holding Robbie's hand (much to his annoyance) followed and Big Roy himself, with Cailean at his side, took up the rear.

'That's the first hurdle safely past,' Jandy was reflecting as she heard the door close behind them but to her dismay this was directly followed by their first piece of bad luck.

Just as they began to move along the 'bankie', with any slight noise they made being drowned by the general din of the storm, there was a loud 'squawk' and a large white shape came dive-bombing down towards them only to stop short and wheel skilfully away round, ready for another mock attack.

'Go away, George,' pleaded Jandy, recognizing the peremptory squawk rather than the look of the gull. 'We've no food for you now and you're only drawing attention to us.'

Never having been so neglected in all his pampered life before, the angry sea-gull did not abandon his campaign at once but presently he decided that it was hopeless and he might as well give up. With a last disgusted cry, he veered off and flew away up over the cottage.

Whether or not this incident had any connection with subsequent events, she was never to know for sure but Jandy had her suspicions.

It was a shock to face the icy elements as they left the shelter of the cottage and Jandy gave a gasp as the first gust of rain-laden wind lashed her face.

'At least,' she reflected, 'I can make as much fuss as I like out here. No-one could hear me even if I screamed.'

53

This thought had rather frightening implications however and she quickly dismissed it.

It took the children all their time to keep their feet in the face of the buffeting of the storm and to hurry was out of the question.

'Keep close to the houses,' John had said and certainly by doing that they obtained some shelter from the weather. What he had not reckoned on was the hazard of having to negotiate all the various obstacles around the cottage doors. There were garden seats and sink gardens and any number of other homely objects, dear to the hearts of Gowrie house-holders and so useful in summer, but such a nuisance now. The little group picked their way carefully round these but there were several minor accidents. Not all the Highlanders were so surefooted as Big Roy.

What with the darkness, the wind and the rain, Jandy had a full-time job looking after herself although she did her best to help Robbie by ushering him in front of her and keeping a firm hold of his belt. It was a great comfort to know that the two Highlanders were behind her in case things should go wrong.

She was concentrating hard on the path at her feet, trying to keep her mind from dwelling on the incredible situation in which they had landed, when Robbie uttered a yelp and, twisting himself from her grasp, darted round her before she could regain a hold on him and ran back the way they had come.

'My ball!' his voice came back to her. 'I've dropped my good luck ball!'

In the confusion of trying to catch him, Jandy and the two Highlanders caught each other and that gave the little boy a few minutes' start on them. In a panic, Jandy ran after him, calling his name and feeling a sense of hopelessness as her words were blown back in her face by the gale. She stumbled

54

a dozen times on the slippery stones of the path and, added to her fears for her little brother, came the awful dread of falling and spraining her own ankle.

Then everything happened at once. The big Jacobite, who was not far ahead of her, had almost caught up with Robbie who was down on all fours, or so it looked to Jandy, probably feeling around for his precious ball when suddenly another shape—larger and more sinister—loomed out from the gap between two cottages nearby.

'Got you, you little devil!' sounded a man's voice and that, plus Robbie's yell of fright, spurred Jandy's weary legs on to further effort. Her knees threatened to give way at each step and yet she kept going somehow until, that is, just as she reached the spot where she thought Robbie must be she felt a hard grip on her shoulder. It was too dark to see who was responsible for this but she was at once aware that she was in the hands of the enemy.

What to do now? Conflicting thoughts raced through her mind. She must get away—but this was one way of finding Robbie—must let Big Roy know where she was—how to do it?

'I'll shout to him,' she decided in desperation and, opening her mouth, tried to call his name but although she strained her hardest no sound came.

'Come on, my fine fellow,' said a far from friendly voice in her ear. 'Let's see how brave you gallant Highlanders are now!'

Surprisingly, having previously been utterly exhausted, Jandy now found that a combination of fear and rage at having been caught had given her new life. She was being half-led, half-dragged into the passageway between the houses but she astonished even herself by the amount of resistance she was able to put up. The oaths of her captor showed that it astonished him too.

'Will you come quietly, you young savage,' said the voice again, 'or must I teach you some manners?'

There was a note of menace in the low voice that made Jandy suddenly realize that perhaps it was foolish to antagonize the Redcoat needlessly. She had no wish to be injured by him and if he was angry he was scarcely likely to be merciful. Robbie might be hurt too. Accordingly she ceased to struggle and submitted to being thrust ahead of the soldier back the way she had come, along the well-trodden path where she had walked free of care so often, past the familiar houses of old neighbours, past—was this really happening?—yes, past No. 63 itself and on.

'Where can he be taking me?' she wondered drearily. 'Surely he's not going up on to Carron Head?' This was the impassable headland which blocked the through road at the east end of the village. Once or twice only, in the height of summers past, she had tried to climb to the top of this great hump of rocky hill with John but she had never reached anywhere near the summit. Her courage had always failed her as soon as she became aware that she was directly above the sea with nothing on the bare, precipitous slope below to save her should she fall.

'If he is going to climb up there,' it occurred to her with a slight feeling of hope, 'he can't possibly keep his hold on me. Maybe I'll have a chance to get away.'

However the Redcoat had no intention of doing anything so obliging. As Jandy was planning how she could give him the slip on the hill she felt once more a rough push and heard the curt command, 'In here and that quickly.'

Although the wind had fallen considerably by this time, the rain was still teeming down steadily and Jandy was so miserably wet that it was a positive relief to see that she was being propelled towards a building of some sort. There were not many houses between No. 63 and the headland and she strained her eyes to see which of these this was. At first she could discern nothing, so unceremoniously was she being pushed forward. She stumbled up a few steps, nearly falling as she did so, and through a door at the top.

'Who goes there?' a voice demanded from the darkness inside the doorway.

'An Englishman and a true subject of King George,' came the answer from Jandy's captor.

'Ah, 'tis you Richard?' asked the sentry, turning the beam of a lamp which must have been covered until then on the two who had entered.

Jandy blinked in the sudden brightness and blinked again as she recognized with a jolt of the heart that she was in the Hall where so lately she had sat enjoying the Anniversary Concert.

'That looks a sullen creature that you have captured this time,' went on the sentry.

Jandy's temper, never very placid, could not take this insult meekly. What really roused her anger however was the sight of a woebegone little figure sitting hunched up in a corner just beyond the door. Piteous sobs were coming from it.

'How dare you speak to me like that!' she cried. 'If this is the behaviour of King George's men, I'll always be a Jacobite. At least we know how to treat women and children!'

The fact that twelve hours before she would scarcely have known what a Jacobite was, quite escaped her mind for the moment. She pulled herself impatiently from the grasp of the soldier and ran over to the crouching Robbie.

'What's wrong, Rob?' she asked, putting a protective arm round him. 'Have the cruel beasts been hurting you?'

A strangled sob was the only reply to this. The two Redcoats in the meantime were conferring in undertones at

57

the door, glancing over at the two Turnbulls every now and then with puzzled looks.

Jandy was quite unaware of this for she was more concerned in case Robbie had been badly hurt.

'Where is the sore place, dear?' she said, using language in the stress of the moment that both she and Robbie would have considered unbearably sloppy in normal circumstances.

'There isn't any sore place,' gulped Robbie. 'I'm just miserable.'

'Because you're so cold and frightened?' said Jandy sympathetically.

'No!' said her brother, gulping no longer but quite indignant at this slight on his boyhood. 'It's because I've lost my good stone ball. He pulled me away just as I was going to pick it up.' He gestured towards the Redcoat with a look of dislike.

Jandy heaved a sigh of relief. If that was all that was worrying him, her little brother could not have been too badly treated. His next words were even more reassuring.

'I wish you would take your arm away, Jandy,' he said. 'It's awfully cissy.'

His sister complied hastily.

'I'm sorry,' she apologized. 'I just thought that you had been badly hurt by these horrible men. They're the sort of people who killed Mary Johnston's family, you know.'

Far from making him nervous, this seemed to interest Robbie and comfort him greatly.

'Just like the story?' he asked and Jandy realized that this to him was not a story coming frighteningly true but the very reverse. The terrors of the present were less frightening because they were part of a familiar and well-loved story.

The two soldiers had now finished their discussion and the one called Richard came over to the children.

The Redcoats' Prison

Something in the way the Redcoat approached them, quietly and almost nervously, made Jandy look up enquiringly. His manner had subtly changed, become gentler and less aggressive.

'By your speech, you are not of the Highland breed,' he began and his voice had none of the brusqueness it had held when he had spoken to Jandy earlier. 'What bond have you with these treasonous clansmen who threaten the peace of our realm?'

'I don't know what you mean,' said Jandy stubbornly. She was not going to be won over by these honeyed tones when the previous harshness was so vivid in her mind. 'What clansmen?'

'Those who sought refuge in your house this night,' replied the soldier. 'We know that they came here and we thought that some of their kinsmen had given them shelter, but 'tis clear that you are not of that wild stock who live among the mountains and speak only the heathenish tongue called Gaelic.'

'No,' retorted Jandy, 'I don't speak Gaelic but,' she added defiantly, 'I wish I did. We haven't seen any savages in Gowrie tonight—except for yourselves, that is. I think it's very savage to attack a little boy and a girl! Especially when they've done you no harm.'

Her voice rose as her indignation grew. The sound brought the sentry over to give support to his comrade.

'What ails the lass?' he asked. 'Have you learnt the whereabouts of the MacIans from her?'

'Not yet,' said the other impatiently. 'I fear she is either a fool or a traitor. She denies any knowledge of the Highlanders but she has an impudent tongue and I mistrust her.'

'Yet 'twould help us mightily if we could have her on our side. Be careful how you deal with her, Rick, lest she turn against us fully and we gain no intelligence.'

A grunt was Rick's only reply to this. Then he addressed himself to Jandy again.

''Twas not our intent to harm you,' he said, 'and I crave your pardon if you or the boy have been hurt. We are seeking some desperate men who are traitors to our King and we believed that you were their kin.'

'What have these men done?' enquired Jandy.

'They are Jacobites who have fought against the rightful King and sought to put in his place one who would return our land to the hated fold of Rome. If you know aught of them 'tis your duty to tell so that we may take them and rid the land of treachery once and for all.'

Much of this speech was above Jandy's head but the main meaning was clear enough.

'What will you do if you catch them?' Jandy asked, trying to sound casual.

'Some we will despatch by the sword at once but the leader, one Roy MacIan, we are commanded to bring back with us to London. He is a wily rascal and responsible for much of the rebels' success. But his time is short! He will not escape us this time and soon he will be incarcerated in the Tower as befits a traitor.'

Jandy's heart sank as she heard the words, so cold and callous that they made her flesh creep. If anything was needed to harden her determination to help the fugitives escape, this was it. The first step however must be to escape from the hands of the Redcoats herself.

'Still,' she thought, 'until I do have the chance to get away, I may as well see what I can find out from them. It may be useful later.'

'Why don't you go out and search for these Jacobites if you

want them so badly?' she asked in what she hoped sounded an innocent tone.

'We have ten men doing that already,' replied the soldier. 'I have done my part in capturing you and must remain now on guard with Ben.'

Jandy's heart sank. With so many hunting them, what chance of escape had the fugitives? Then with a sickening thud of despair she remembered that it was not only the Jacobites who were being hunted. John and Shona were out there too and in danger. Resolutely, she turned her mind away from that thought.

'But how can you hope to find anyone on a dark night like this? Surely it would be better to wait until morning when it's light.'

'No, for they mean to take ship for France in the morning with the aid of some traitorous scoundrel who had helped many of their kind.'

There was a sudden flurry of rain against the windows just then and an eerie sough of the wind at the same time showed that the storm was rising again to a new pitch. Ben shivered.

'Though 'tis true they are villains,' he muttered, 'yet my heart is sore for them—or for any poor wretch who is out on these hills this night.'

Rick's expression was hidden in the shadows but the snort of disgust with which he greeted this kindly remark was a clear enough indication of how he felt.

'Be thankful then that you are safe in shelter here,' he sneered, 'for you would be of little use in the chase if your thoughts are those of a milk-sop.'

Silence ensued for a time after that. The two men had moved away again, the sentry to his post by the door and Rick to the window where his figure could dimly be seen striving vainly to see out. Then, with an exclamation of impatience he turned away from it.

'Where can those laggards be?' he cried. ''Tis not so large a town that they must have a whole night to search it. Do you keep watch over these two, Ben, and I shall seek the rest of our troop for it bodes ill for us all if we do not bring in our quarry.'

As he spoke, he strode across the room and Jandy could see him, in the glow of the sentry's lamp, grasping the door-handle. At the same instant the door burst open and a new figure entered, shaking the rain from him like a dog and gasping with the effort of struggling against the wind. Whoever he was, the newcomer was obviously a welcome sight to Rick at least.

'Well met, Thomas,' he cried. 'How goes the search?'

There was relief in his voice as he no doubt saw himself being saved a journey out in the cold but the reply he got was hardly encouraging.

'That I do not know,' replied the other, 'for I lost sight of them when we parted to carry on the pursuit singly—for in truth we were proceeding so slowly.'

'Then why came you back?' asked Rick, enraged by such slackness.

'Why to be sure I thought they must have found the rebels and I looked to see them back here again. For truly, what could I do alone?'

'Well, now you can remain here and bear Ben company. I shall go and seek the rest of our troop.'

He went then, banging the door behind him. The noise woke Robbie who had long since fallen asleep and he asked drowsily, 'Is it time to get up?'

'What have you there?' asked the soldier Thomas curiously, approaching the corner where the two Turnbulls were sitting. Instinctively Jandy shrank back and put a protective arm round Robbie again as the sentry's lamp was flashed in her face.

'Two of the peasants of this place,' said Ben carelessly. 'Rick brought them here some while back, hoping to learn something of the Jacobites from them. But they told nothing. The boy is too young and the maid too stubborn.'

'Maid?' echoed the other in surprise. 'She is garbed as no maid I have seen!'

'What else do you expect in these wild regions!' laughed the sentry. 'But enough of them,' he went on, drawing Thomas away. 'I have a matter here to interest you more.'

For a moment Jandy wondered what this could be but the sound of noisy drinking and the smacking of lips soon told her. Alternating feelings of hope and fear flitted through her mind as she listened. Would they drink themselves into a befuddled state or would they turn violent with it? If the former, she had perhaps some chance of making her getaway but if the latter—she did not want to pursue that train of thought. However, just in case, she decided to make sure that Robbie stayed awake this time for no matter what effect the drink had, they would probably have to act fast when the crucial moment came.

'Stand up and stretch yourself, Rob,' she whispered. 'We may have to run soon and you won't be able to if your legs are stiff with sitting.'

'Where will we run to?' asked Robbie with interest. The idea of escaping did not seem to have occurred to him.

'Ho there, lass,' came a voice, before Jandy had a chance to reply to this and her heart took a plunge as she realized that the soldier had probably heard her words to her little brother. Now he would be on his guard against any escape attempt. She could have kicked herself!

' 'Tis a dreary plight for a young lass like yourself to be prisoned here with none but a child for company. Will you not come over here and join us? At least we can offer light and good cheer and there's warmth in the bottle too,' went on the speaker and Jandy recognized the accents of the soldier Thomas.

Fearful of offending him by refusing this invitation, Jandy rose and made to go over with Robbie as she was bidden. She was surprised how cramped her legs felt and how cold the room was, now that she was on her feet.

'I must have been numb without realizing it,' she thought. 'It's just as well I got up.'

A Friend in Disguise

The two men moved over to make room for them on their benches which Jandy recognized as the very seats they had all sat on at the concert. Could that really have been only a few hours ago? To Jandy it seemed more like years and she certainly felt she was much older than she had been the evening before.

She politely refused the rather unwholesome-looking bottle which Ben amiably held out for her to sample.

'Not thirsty?' he repeated in surprise as if he could hardly believe such a thing. 'But this spirit does more than satisfy thirst—it also brings comfort to the heart. Why, the sound of the storm without there, makes the very blood freeze in my veins and a drink from this helps to warm it up again.'

'Aye,' agreed Thomas, 'there is a sadness in the howling of the wind that brings to mind the cries of lost souls. What think ye, Ben? Are these the spirits of men we slew at Culloden Moor? Or have dwellers in this town from long past times come back to warn us away?'

Ben shuddered and hastily took another drink.

'Do not speak so,' he begged. 'Ill luck comes on those who talk of such matters. Oh, would that this long night would pass and we should all be safe back among our comrades!'

'You speak wisely,' said Thomas. 'Let us therefore sing and make merry so that we may forget the terrors of the night.'

This was something that exactly suited Robbie. He loved singing and had a surprisingly good ear for a tune as well as a retentive memory for the words. (Unfortunately, this did not extend to more everyday matters, like schoolwork.)

'I know a good song,' he volunteered. 'You can help me, Jandy.' And to his sister's horror he launched without more ado into 'Charlie is my Darling', one of the songs he had heard at the concert the evening before.

Jandy did not know what to do. The two Englishmen might not recognize the song but if they listened to the words they would soon realize that it was a Jacobite one. Luckily, on this occasion Robbie had not picked up the words very well and after a few lines she was able to suggest that he change to something else that he knew better.

So the next half-hour or so was passed pleasantly in singing twentieth century pop songs with two English Redcoats. Ben joined in lustily and the more he sang, the more recourse he had to his bottle. The result of this was as might have been expected. One moment the sentry was in full voice joining in the singing, the next he had toppled over and lay sound asleep on the floor.

'Poor fellow,' said Thomas, looking at the sprawling figure of his friend. 'I hope he is not beset by ghosts and spectres in his dreams.'

Privately Jandy thought, 'It will be mostly your fault if he is.' But she said nothing. She did not really trust Thomas for there was something odd about him that she could not quite place. Rick was hard and ruthless, Ben seemed more like a

65

simple countryman than a soldier but this man was not like either of them. It was not that he was unpleasant—quite the reverse—but more that there was something phoney about him.

'Now,' he said briskly, turning to Jandy, 'there is little time for courtesies and much has to be accomplished before this night is through. Know you where Roy MacIan is to be found?'

'Roy MacIan?' stammered Jandy, too taken aback by the directness of the question to dodge it. 'N-no, I've been shut up here with Robbie for hours.'

'But you were with MacIan earlier, were you not?'

Jandy nodded, feeling that she was not really giving anything away by admitting this. After all, the Jacobites could be anywhere by now. Then she received another surprise.

'Do not be afraid to tell me,' said the Redcoat. 'I may wear an English soldier's coat but my heart is with the Jacobite cause. I joined the King's force so that I might supply information to the Prince.'

Jandy looked at him with a new feeling of respect. She did not altogether approve of spies but there was no denying that it took courage to be one.

'That must be very dangerous,' she said, 'but what are you going to do now that the Prince has been defeated?'

'I have to do what I can to help the Highlanders reach safety. Some are able to return to their homes but the leaders have to leave this country and hope to find refuge in France. That is why I seek Roy MacIan now.'

It did not occur to Jandy to question the truth of the man's claims. She had been aware that there was something 'wrong' about him and of course so there would be if he was always playing a part.

'We were helping Big Roy and his friends to escape when

66

Robbie and I were caught. I don't know what happened after that. I just hope the others got away safely.'

'The rest of your friends are safe,' replied Thomas—really the man was full of surprises! 'but they have not left the town. Only Big Roy is missing and his men would not leave without him.'

'Have you seen my brother and sister?' asked Jandy eagerly. 'Can you take us to them?'

'Yes,' replied the soldier. 'That is where we are going now, if you are able to walk. As we go, I shall tell you what must be done.'

They crept towards the door as silently as they could, considering the difficulty of doing so, what with the bare wooden floor-boards and the poor light available. The storm was still audible outside and Ben appeared to be sound asleep but even so, they did not want to take any risks.

'Wait here until I return to tell you that it is safe to follow,' whispered Thomas as he closed the door of the Hall behind them. ''Twould serve our venture ill should we be seen by Rick.'

The children stood waiting miserably. Not only was there a constant drip of outsize raindrops from the eaves under which they were trying to gain some shelter but the passageway in which they stood served as a funnel up which the wind blew with even greater force than it did in the open.

'I wish we had stayed inside with Ben,' said Robbie plaintively. 'That was good fun.'

Luckily Thomas returned just then to tell them that the coast was clear and they were able to move away from their uncomfortable position.

Once more they faced the wind and rain driving in from the sea. Thomas had told Robbie to hold on to his belt and Jandy kept a grip on her little brother's shoulders but this arrangement presented its own problems. Robbie's short legs

67

could not keep up with the long strides of the soldier and Jandy, try as she might, could not keep in step with Robbie. She kept treading on his heels and bumping into him, to the great discomfort of both.

The only benefit of the bad weather was that it drowned the noise they made for, with so much else to guard against, it was quite impossible to proceed quietly.

They had passed No. 63 where Jandy gazed longingly at the familiar orange door and wondered if she would ever see the inside of it again and they were close to the spot where Robbie had been caught when Thomas suddenly halted and turned to issue an urgent warning.

'There is someone before us on the road,' he said in a low tone. 'Be as still as you can and he may pass unaware of us.'

'I think there's a gap between the houses just about here. Could we not go in there?' whispered Jandy, recognizing where they were.

This seemed a good idea and, by feeling their way along the wall, they located the gap and all three slipped into it.

It was as well that they had done this for very shortly afterwards there came the sound of heavy treads advancing along the path towards them. Thomas must have sensed the stranger's presence earlier by some special instinct of his own for until that moment Jandy had heard nothing. Now the listeners froze as the footsteps approached, fearing to betray their presence by some involuntary movement. There was a lull in the storm just then which made it seem that the whole world was listening too in the unnatural silence.

Then to the horror of the three standing there pressed hard against the cottage wall, the footsteps faltered and came to a halt right beside their hiding-place.

A Surprise Meeting

Jandy held her breath and at the same time placed a warning hand over Robbie's mouth to prevent him from saying anything. This was an involuntary action on her part which she later denied having done when indignantly challenged by her little brother.

'Fuirich an seo, mo charaid,'* came a man's voice and the light reflected from the sea was blotted out by a massive shape which loomed up beside them.

Jandy's mouth opened but the scream of terror which was on the way out died on her lips as a sudden thought struck her. She had heard that voice before, although the words it uttered meant nothing to her. At the same instant Robbie let out a cry of joy.

'It's Big Roy, come to save us!'

Obviously their attempts at keeping their presence there a secret had been successful for it was the turn of the Highlander to be surprised. A startled exclamation came from him and at the same time something heavy fell with a thud at the children's feet.

Thomas was quick to size up the situation. After all, he had been looking for this man for a long time and he knew so much about him that he seemed like an old friend.

'What have you there, MacIan?' he asked, bending down as he spoke to give the bundle at his feet an exploratory prod with his finger. Then he straightened again and gave a low whistle. 'That's a strange burden for an honest man to carry.'

Naturally the Jacobite was inclined to be very wary of this stranger who so readily assumed his acquaintance and at first he did not reply. But after Jandy had done her best, with frequent interjections from Robbie, to explain matters he relaxed a little.

*Wait here, my friend.

69

'Tell us what happened to you after we were caught,' begged Jandy. 'Have you seen the others? Are they safe?'

She was going on to add more questions to this list but paused for breath and Big Roy seized his opportunity while he could.

'Hush, young lady,' he said gently. 'You ask so much. If you will listen, I shall tell you all I know.'

It seemed that, after Jandy and Robbie had fallen into the hands of the Redcoats, Roy had hung around the area for a time in the hope of being able to rescue them somehow.

'Young Cailean I sent away to tell the rest of our company what had befallen and to warn my kinsmen to make good their escape alone—for what would it profit our cause were three good men to fall into the enemy's hands for the sake of one?'

After lying in wait for some time, trying to discover what was happening at the Hall, he had finally decided that his only course was to raid the place on his own and hope to take the two captives away by force.

'I set aside my trusty claymore,' he told them, 'and found me a good, stout stick instead for a sword is no weapon for using in the dark. Then, with the stick in one hand and my sgian dhu in the other, I crept up to the house where you were held and made ready to charge the door.'

'We didn't hear a thing,' said Jandy wonderingly.

'And that is how it should be when MacIan is on the trail of a foe. It is only in the heat of battle that we Highlanders cry our slogans as we fight.'

All the while as he spoke, they had been standing huddled together uncomfortably at the spot where they had first all met up. Now, despite her interest in the story, Jandy could not hold back a sudden shiver and at the same time her teeth chattered uncontrollably.

'Here now,' exclaimed Big Roy. 'I will give you my plaid

to wrap round yourself and the boy. The night is wearing on and we must rejoin our comrades if we are to reach Banff in time for the ship tomorrow.'

'Stay a moment,' cried Thomas suddenly. 'I had forgot what I had to tell you. One of the English troopers intercepted a Jacobite messenger this night and persuaded him to tell his errand. It seems that so many of the escaping Jacobites fail to reach their ship in Banff harbour that the captain sails before his time unless he has certain word that more fugitives are on their way.'

'But how can anyone get a message through more quickly than they can travel themselves,' asked Jandy, thinking that she would appreciate the benefit of a telephone more in future. That in turn led to the melancholy afterthought—if I ever see a telephone again.

'By lighting a beacon on one of the headlands,' Thomas replied. 'They will keep a look-out from the town and if a fire appears on any of the surrounding cliff-tops at least one hour before the appointed time for the ship to leave, it will be taken as a sign that the fugitives are on their way.'

'From the look of the sky,' said Roy, 'dawn is fast approaching and we have no time for climbing any hill, no matter what the purpose. We have taken many risks in these past months and one more will not trouble us.'

''Twas my intent to light the beacon for you,' said Thomas. 'It would be hard indeed were you to make the hazardous journey to Banff and there to find your ship already gone. I would have gone long since but had to be assured that you were indeed still on your way.'

'John knows the way up Carron Head,' volunteered Jandy. 'He climbs it every summer. He'll be able to tell you the best way to go.'

'Good,' returned the soldier. 'Then we must make all haste to find him—but what of your prisoner? Mean you to leave him here?' The last words were addressed to Roy and Jandy realized that they referred to the 'bundle' that the Jacobite had been carrying when he first came up to them.

She had been aware for some time of faint moaning sounds coming from the thing at her feet but, not having her sister's talent for nursing, had not known what to do about them. Now she wondered who the prisoner was.

'I care not what becomes of him,' answered Roy. 'He is of no use to me now although I had thought to use him as a ransom against the release of my young friends here. I might have cast him into the sea long since—' Jandy suppressed a gasp at this '—but had no stomach for the deed. That is how the Redcoats deal with their prisoners but it is not my way.'

'But who is he and how did you capture him?' asked Jandy curiously.

'Before I could storm the place where you were held captive,' said Big Roy, 'this man came out and I saw by the light of a lamp shining within that he was one of the English troopers. I did not wish to attack him there lest some of his comrades should hear and come to his aid. So I followed him for some way and then I fell upon him. He fought bravely but I quickly gained the mastery.'

'It must be Rick,' thought Jandy. 'It was his fault that we were caught in the first place. Still, I wouldn't like to leave him here to die of exposure.'

Aloud she said, 'Why don't we cover him with this cloak since we can't do much to help him? Maybe some of his friends will find him before long.'

'Little did I think that I would use my plaid to help a Redcoat,' murmured Roy, but he helped her to wrap it round the Englishman all the same.

They left him then and continued their slow progress along the path, looking for John and the others. This time Thomas hoisted Robbie on to his back and he led the way with Jandy and Roy following. As they went along, Jandy fell to wondering again how her brother and sister had fared. Roy had not mentioned them and had obviously had no contact with the rest of the group since sending Cailean away to join them.

'For all we know,' thought Jandy, 'there may have been more Redcoats waiting to catch them and they could all be prisoners at this very moment.'

In this she was wrong, however. Although her brother and sister had been through some nerve-racking experiences since she had last seen them, they had never been in danger of imprisonment. Quite the reverse, in fact.

Along the Bankie

As John led the little group away from No. 63, he was filled with a mixture of elation and foreboding: elation at being able to do something active at last after the hours of nail-biting indecision, foreboding at whatever hazards this sortie into the unknown might bring.

'I hope we can find somewhere to shelter a while,' he thought, 'so that we can have a chance to think out some sort of plan. I don't fancy being in charge of the Jacobites when they don't seem to speak much English—not without Big Roy, at any rate.'

As before, the going was rough but the storm had dropped somewhat—or perhaps he was just getting used to it. Whatever the reason, they made quite good progress and John found himself about half-way to the burn before very long. (He was not to know that, even before this, both

Robbie and Jandy had fallen into the Redcoats' hands.)

'Hallo,' he said to himself, seeing a faint glow inside the window of the cottage he was then passing—a window where no light should have been. 'Someone's in there. I wonder if a tramp has broken in to find shelter from the storm. I suppose I ought to go in and see what he's up to.'

He flashed his torch, which he had been using very sparingly in an effort to save the battery, back up the way he had come. The others were nowhere to be seen, not surprisingly as the visibility was poor.

'No use waiting for them,' he reflected. 'This chap could set the place ablaze with a dropped match any minute. I only hope he doesn't turn nasty.'

He was in some doubt as to whether he really had any right to follow the intruder into the house but he knew that the owners would be away for the winter and it did not seem likely that the man with the light had any more right there than he.

Thinking over this incident later, John marvelled at his own stupidity. He knew that the visitors of the night were Jacobites who had strayed two and a half centuries ahead of their time and he was quite convinced that they were being pursued by English Redcoats who were solid enough to knock stones down the hillside yet it still did not occur to him that the mystery man in the cottage was anything other than an ordinary tramp.

He was soon to have the truth brought home to him. As he braced himself to go into the cottage, mentally rehearsing what he would say, he felt his arm being gripped from behind and an excited flood of talk was poured into his ear. He recognized the voice of Domhnull but before he had time to say anything the light in the cottage shone again. This time it showed the face of the man who was striking it.

'Funny-looking tramp!' thought John but still the truth did not dawn on him.

74

Aloud he said to the Highlander, 'I'm going in there to find out who that is and what he's doing.'

'Do not go!' cried Domhnull, grabbing his arm again. 'Do you not see that he is one of the Cotaichean Dearga—the English soldiers?'

As he spoke he tried to pull John away from the spot. Despite himself, John could not help being infected by his agitation although he still could not take his fears quite seriously.

'What would an English soldier be doing in the Stewarts' house?' he asked.

'They are looking for us,' returned the other, 'and for Ruaidh Mor most of all.'

'Better humour the poor chap,' thought John. 'He's been through so much, he's starting to imagine things.'

He put the thought of the man in the cottage out of his head after that for now the need for some place to shelter was really pressing. Just as he was reaching a point of desperation, his attention was caught by a curious squeaking sound that could be clearly heard even amid the lashing of the rain and the constant surge of the waves.

Once more he risked a quick flash of his torch and saw to his joy that the noise came from the swinging door of Mr Menzies' big shed. It had obviously been blown open by the gale and now hung invitingly ajar, squeaking loudly every time the wind gusted. John stepped inside. Good, it was fine and dry here. The rain had only soaked the floor around the entrance and the shed was quite roomy enough to accommodate them all with ease.

The owner of the place was a fisherman, although nowadays he only worked in the summer months, and this was where he kept all his nets and tackle of all sorts. Fish boxes too were stacked up against the wall.

John chuckled to himself as he stood there waiting for the

others to come along. There was a double pleasure in finding this particular door open. None of the Turnbulls had ever been in Mr Menzies' shed before for the old man did not exactly welcome visitors. He especially disapproved of the holiday families and the younger members of the community steered well clear of him as a result.

'I wonder what old Menzies would say if he could see us in his precious store-room?' thought John. 'Just wait till Jandy sees where we are!'

He hugged the thought to himself, comfortable in the knowledge that there was no fear of the old man finding them as he always spent the winter months with his married daughter in Aberdeen nowadays.

He began to investigate the contents of the store while he waited but had only time for a quick survey before Domhnull came in, attracted by the glow of his torch. His first act was to shake himself like a dog so that the spray flew out in all directions around him.

'Hey!' exclaimed John. 'Mind what you're doing! Don't you think I'm wet enough already?'

He gave the Jacobite a friendly but firm push so that he subsided suddenly on one of the packing-cases that littered the shed. Both he and John began to laugh at this un-expected turn of events and for the first time something like genuine fellow-feeling sprang up between them. Into this happy atmosphere came Iain Ban accompanied by Shona and Hamish. It was actually the dog who had followed their trail and led the other two after him for John had quite forgotten to keep a look-out.

'Are the other three far behind you, do you know?' John asked Shona when the new arrivals had settled down in various corners.

'No idea,' she said, 'but I bet Robbie is holding them back. Where are we going after this, John? We really ought to be getting a move on if they're going to walk to Banff tonight.' She nodded towards their Jacobite companions as she spoke though of course this was lost on John as the darkness in the shed was total.

'We can't do much till Big Roy arrives,' replied her brother. 'So far as I can see, though, the only way to go is up the side of the burn until it's narrow enough to cross. That could mean a walk of miles. So I think you and Robbie should stay behind here with Jandy.'

'If you want Hamish to go with you—' began Shona but she broke off to listen as a sudden commotion broke out back up the village from where they had just come.

'What on earth!' exclaimed John as the unmistakable sound of breaking glass mingled with strident human voices.

'They've had some kind of accident,' cried Shona in alarm. 'We'd better go and help them!'

An hour earlier John would have agreed to this suggestion at once but the incident of the intruder in the cottage had taught him caution. Were those really the voices of the other Jacobites or were the villagers across in Wester Gowrie calling to one another? Or—incredible thought, were there English soldiers in the village, perhaps searching the houses for their friends?

'Wait a minute,' John said sharply, laying a restraining hand on Shona's arm. 'Keep quiet till we listen'

'Why, what do you think is happening?' whispered Shona. 'Why can't we go out to see?'

'You're not going to understand this,' answered John, 'but take my word for it. There are English soldiers in the village and they're after Big Roy and his friends.'

He paused dramatically to let this sink in but was a little disappointed by Shona's casual reaction.

'Are these the Redcoats everyone was talking about? Of course, I know about them.'

'Well,' demanded her brother, 'do you want the Jacobites to be caught—for that's what will happen if we go running about the place trying to find Jandy and Big Roy. We must think out the best way to go so that the Redcoats won't be suspicious.'

'What we really want,' replied Shona, 'is to get them out of the way so that Jandy can get along here safely. That's right, isn't it?'

'Well, yes,' said her brother, 'but that's easier said than done.'

Shona's Story

They lapsed into thoughtful silence, racking their brains for some solution to the problem. A short, sharp bark from Hamish startled them all to their feet. John's torch revealed the dog standing, ears erect and nose pressed against the crack of the door and the two Highlanders beside him, poised ready to tackle whoever or whatever had alerted the dog.

As he switched off the light again, John fancied that he saw the door start to open slowly. A tell-tale squeak told him that he had not been mistaken. Then a voice spoke and Domhnull's response told him that the newcomer was a friend.

'Am I glad to see you?' cried John thankfully, switching on his torch again. 'What kept—?' His voice faltered as he saw that Cailean stood there alone.

'Where are Robbie and Jandy?' asked Shona in alarm.

It was Domhnull who eventually got the story from his fellow Jacobite and then told it to the others. The two

Turnbulls heard him out in silence but despair grew in their hearts as they listened.

'But have no fear,' Domhnull finished. 'Ruaidh Mor will save them.'

John sank down on one of the packing cases and rested his head gloomily in his hands. He only roused himself for a moment when a sudden thought occurred to him.

'Did Cailean see any soldiers?' he asked. 'How did he get past them?'

'He says that he saw no-one,' Domhnull told him, 'but he heard them as they went about their devil's work.'

'They must have been inside one of the cottages,' said Shona. Then she cried eagerly, 'That's what we must do— we'll trap them inside—up in the loft would be best!'

'And just how do you suggest we do that?' asked her brother scornfully. 'Unless of course I just walk up to a soldier and say, ''Would you care to step up into the loft for a moment. I'd like you to stay there, out of my way!'''

'Don't be silly,' retorted Shona. 'They'd never do it for you. You're too old. But they'd trust me if I asked them—if I said that I thought the Jacobites were hiding up there.'

Shona was so enthusiastic about this daring scheme that she could not keep quiet and kept talking about it.

John was still sceptical but he was willing to discuss the idea if only to keep his mind occupied. Domhnull listened eagerly too and reported their conversation to his two comrades.

In the end they thrashed out some sort of plan and lost no time in putting it into practice.

So it was that some time later when Thomas and Robbie, Jandy and Big Roy came along looking for them, they heard an excited voice hailing them from the shadows.

'In here, quick! Domhnull and Cailean are guarding the Redcoats in the Stewarts' cottage but the rest of us are in here.'

Shona launched into her account of what had happened almost before the newcomers had found places for themselves in the shed.

Waiting until the English soldiers were coming down the road, fresh from ransacking houses farther along, she had gone to meet them, pretending to be very excited.

'I told them I thought there were Jacobite traitors hiding in the cottage and I said I'd heard strange noises coming from it. John had gone up to the loft earlier and left Domhnull's tammy there in a corner where they would be sure to find it when they searched.

'They all trooped into the house and began to turn the living-room upside down.'

'Weren't you scared?' asked Jandy.

'Well,' replied Shona consideringly, 'I had Hamish there to protect me and the others were quite nearby. They were waiting for me to give them the signal that the soldiers were all up in the loft.

'Anyway, while I was standing there, I suddenly heard the sound of somebody moving about overhead. I nearly died for there shouldn't have been anyone there. The soldiers heard it too and made a dive for the ladder up to the loft.

'The next second there was a yell from upstairs and then there was a noise as if someone had jumped down from the loft and I felt something brush past my leg.'

'What did you do?' asked Robbie. 'I bet you screamed!'

'Why should I?' asked his sister. 'I knew it was only Tibby for she let out one big miaow as she ran past.'

'Don't ask how she got up there,' put in John at this point. 'Iain Ban didn't even know she'd gone but it was a stroke of luck for us because it got all the soldiers up into the loft and gave Domhnull and me the chance to nip in and take the ladder away.'

'But surely the Redcoats can easily escape. All they need to

80

do is to jump down. These rooms aren't very high,' remarked Jandy.

'I don't think they will, somehow,' said John, grinning. 'They don't seem to like the look of the two Jacobites down below. I don't know whether it's Domhnull's gun or Cailean's dirk that discourages them but something does.'

Jandy shuddered. This evening was becoming too bloodthirsty for comfort.

'Well,' John continued, 'now that you're here there's nothing to keep us. We can start to try and find our way up by the burn-side to reach the Banff road. I don't think you should come, though, Jandy. You'd be better to stay here with the youngsters.'

'But suppose the Redcoats get away,' objected Jandy. 'They will probably be so mad that they'll take it out on us— and the house too, most likely.'

'Oh come off it,' scoffed her brother. 'Surely you could keep out of their way and they will hardly damage the houses—not intentionally, anyway. Isn't that so, Roy?'

'It is not just damage that they will be doing,' replied the other. 'When they are angered they care not what they do. They will even vent their rage by burning the houses. That is ever their way, as I have cause to know.'

The last words were so quietly spoken that John could barely hear them. He longed to know the story behind them but hesitated to ask. There was such suppressed anger in the man's voice, but sorrow and hopelessness too, that to press him seemed an intrusion. However, after a moment he continued without prompting.

'The battle was over and we knew that our cause was lost. The Prince had taken to the hills and his loyal troops were left to find their own way to their homes. I, with Domhnull here and Cailean and Iain Ban, succeeded in getting away from the battlefield without encountering any of the

81

Sassenach wretches who had been set on to us and after a long and weary journey we reached our native glen.'

He paused to regain control of his voice which was trembling with emotion at the recollection.

'What did you find there?' asked John. 'Had the Redcoats been to look for you?'

'We found ruin there and desolation and murder,' replied Roy. 'The dastards had come when no men were there to protect the women and children—aye, and the old folks. Not finding us whom they sought, they had wreaked their hatred on the weak. My children and my parents were lying murdered and our houses were naught but smouldering heaps of stone.'

'And was your wife all right?' asked John.

'They must have carried her off with them,' the Highlander said quietly. 'She and the youngest bairn had gone, leaving no sign to show where I should seek them.'

John felt that nothing he could say would be fitting at such a moment. He searched in his mind for words of sympathy but anything he thought of sounded hollow and futile. Then he had an inspiration.

'If you escape to France,' he said, 'you will meet lots of your Jacobite friends, won't you? So that will give you a chance to find out about your family.'

Roy mumbled some sort of agreement.

'Well,' John concluded, 'the sooner you get on your way for Banff, the better.'

'True,' said the Highlander, 'there are many of our clan in that country already. To reach Banff is the first step in joining them. The good provost has sympathy for our cause and has helped many fugitives to escape under the very noses of the English who hold his town.'

'Good,' said John briskly, 'then let's go.'

'There's just one thing, I'm afraid,' put in Jandy. 'The

boat won't wait for them indefinitely. Thomas will tell you all about it.'

Thomas was introduced and related the tale of how a beacon must be lit to inform the people at Banff.

'Since you know the way up Carron Head,' said Jandy as he finished, 'I thought you might give Thomas some advice about the best route to take.'

'That's a bit tricky,' said John thoughtfully. 'I don't see how I can help you much. In the dark you won't be able to see any landmarks for instance. I really think,' he added slowly, 'that I'd be best to see to the beacon myself and you can help the others get away from here.'

The decision had to be made quickly for time was precious now and since John was the experienced climber, it was generally agreed that he should be the one to light the beacon. And after the dreadful tale of what had happened to Roy's family, John quite agreed that the other Turnbulls should take their chance with the fugitives rather than wait behind in the village.

'Besides,' Shona remarked, 'I don't want to meet the Redcoats, after what I did to them.'

Only a few details remained to be settled. After John had started the beacon fire he was to try and meet up with the others, assuming that they had managed to reach the main road. It was Jandy who suggested this for she did not feel capable of advising the Highlanders on how to cope with present-day traffic and she thought John would be better equipped.

'I'll be off, then,' said John, keen to get started now that it was all fixed. 'See you all again as soon as I can make it.'

And, pulling the waterproof hood of his kagoule up over his head once more, he plunged out into the night.

The Way to Banff

Left behind in the shed, the rest of the party were now preparing for their own journey, mentally at least, since there was not much they could actually do.

'I think the best course will be for me to go ahead,' said Thomas, 'and spy out the way for the rest of you. One man can travel more quickly than a company.'

'Two men are better still,' Big Roy pointed out, 'for the lone traveller may meet with ill fortune and need the aid of another. Therefore I shall go with you.'

Jandy had the feeling that his motive was not solely a desire to be of help to Thomas. She had the sneaking suspicion that Big Roy did not altogether trust this Redcoat-turned-Jacobite-sympathizer.

'What do you want us to do?' she enquired. 'Do we wait here for your return or follow after you in ten minutes or so?'

'We shall return,' said the Highlander, 'when we have traced the first part of the way.'

It did cross Jandy's mind that she might offer him the use of John's torch which he had generously left behind for her but she decided against doing so in the end. They might not trust such a modern gadget and it could affect their trust of her. Anyway Big Roy, at least, seemed to be able to get around like a cat in the dark.

Thinking this, Jandy wondered where their own cat was. Hamish could be heard pottering about, snuffling into all the corners of the shed but Tibby—? She flicked on the torch for a moment and satisfied herself that the cat was back, safely asleep, on Robbie's lap.

Shona and Robbie were sitting back-to-back, like bookends and they too were dozing. This was too much for Jandy and she felt her own eyelids drooping, no matter how she told herself that it was vital to remain alert. Suddenly Hamish's aimless sniffing became more purposeful as was obvious from the noise he was making. Idly, Jandy wondered what he had found but decided against switching on the light to find out. Then such a din broke out that she could no longer ignore it. Barks from Hamish and cries of surprise from Iain Ban were mingled with yells from Robbie.

'What on earth's happening?' asked Jandy testily, for her temper had been sorely tried by the night's adventures.

She switched on the torch, meaning to quell the noisy ones with a glare but instead, the sight which met her eyes made her gasp. Where the back wall of the shed had been before there was now a gaping hole and through it drifted a cold draught of faintly musty air. This was the more noticeable as the shed had gradually been growing more and more stuffy.

'What happened?' repeated Jandy, this time in genuine enquiry.

Iain Ban was in the act of picking himself up from the floor, rubbing his head as he did so and Shona was quietly having hysterics in a corner and neither was capable of giving an account of the last few minutes. However, Jandy gathered that it had all started with Hamish.

'He was sniffing at something just beside me,' said Shona when she had calmed down a little. 'Then he got more excited and began to bark. That's when the mouse ran over my foot and I screamed.'

'And Hamish must've knocked Iain Ban down,' volunteered Robbie, 'for he nearly fell on top of me.'

Iain Ban's lack of English made him unable to tell his part of the story but Jandy guessed that, in falling, he had probably put out a hand instinctively to steady himself against the wall. In doing so he must have touched some hidden spring and so revealed the secret chamber. Thinking that the discovery might prove useful if they wanted a place to hide in a hurry, Jandy shone the torchlight directly on the gap. A few seconds was all she felt she could afford of this for John had impressed the need for conservation on her, but this was long enough to show that what had at first glance appeared to be merely a shallow alcove was actually the beginning of a sizeable passage.

The little group in the shed sat without speaking, struck dumb by awe at the new turn of events. Then into the silence stepped Big Roy and Thomas, much subdued by an unsuccessful trip.

'The stream is running too high for us to cross it,' said the trooper, in answer to Jandy's anxious enquiries. 'We journeyed for a mile or more but it got no better and we knew that we were going in the wrong direction. So we determined to return and seek some other way.'

'We shall try instead to bridge the burn here in the town,' said the Highlander. 'At least the way is paved and firm.'

'Ruaidh Mor,' came the voice of Iain Ban out of the dark and slightly muffled, it seemed. 'Trobhad seo!' (Come here)

Guessing that he wanted to show his leader what had after all been his discovery, Jandy again obliged with a flash of light.

'Do you know anything of this?' whispered Roy, turning to Jandy.

'Not really,' she answered slowly. 'I've often heard that there are smugglers' passages from the old days in the village but nobody ever knew where they were.'

'If this is the work of smugglers,' said the Jacobite, 'it will lead most likely to some spot far from habitation. It may be the answer to our prayers for the way through the clachan is well-nigh impossible.'

'Suppose the passage is blocked though,' objected Jandy. 'It must be years since it was used. We might end up cornered and even more at the mercy of the Redcoats for they will be angry at having walked into our trap.'

Without realizing it, she was even falling into the speech rhythms of the Jacobites. As the others were mulling over her argument there was an unexpected end to the deadlock. A distant 'yip! yip!' coming from goodness knew where reminded Shona that the dog had disappeared but to Roy the sound had another meaning.

'Hark at the dog,' he said. 'He is well away now and is still running. Better for us that we should follow him than stay here, waiting for the soldiers to come and take us.'

Shona was in no doubt about what she felt.

'We must go after Hamish,' she exclaimed. 'He might get lost up there all on his own.'

'All right,' announced Jandy finally, reflecting that it might be less uncomfortable to explore the tunnel than to brave the cold outside again. 'I'll go.'

Iain Ban was despatched to fetch the other two Highlanders from their guard duties and returned with them at his heels in a very short time. He must have impressed them with the need for speed for they had obviously not even delayed long enough to barricade the cottage door so that the troopers would be held back a little longer. The result of this was that they had scarcely closed the shed door behind them before the harsh sound of alien voices was heard outside. The Redcoats, enraged at having been fooled, were bent on vengeance.

'Quickly,' whispered Roy urgently. 'We must take our chance in the tunnel now. The air is fresh enough and there must be some way out to the open. Come!'

Iain Ban took Robbie on his back and Domhnull insisted on doing the same for Shona, despite her protests. The two pets had, of course, long vanished up the tunnel.

'Do you lead the way,' said Roy to Jandy, 'as you have the lamp. I shall stay in the rear to discourage pursuit.'

The words sounded mild enough but there was a note of

menace in the Highlander's tone which struck a chill into Jandy. However she was too busy ushering the others into the passage by torchlight to have time to brood. One by one they stepped in and then Jandy moved to the front of the group, taking the light with her so that the others were left in darkness. Only Roy did not come with them at once for he waited behind in the shed long enough to lug some of the packing-cases over to disguise the hole in the wall, just in case a Redcoat grew inquisitive. Then, this done, he came on behind.

The Jacobites managed the journey up the passage fairly well for they seemed to move as easily in its dark, narrow confines as they had out in the open but for Jandy the next hour was a nightmare. Even with the torch switched on, she could hardly see any distance in front of her feet and she was afraid all the time that even this feeble light would give out. Besides, she was really feeling the effects by now of the long, sleepless night and she had difficulty maintaining what she considered a suitable pace.

The floor of the tunnel was uneven and seemed to slope continuously upwards and Jandy in her exhaustion kept stumbling and having to steady herself by clutching at the rough surface of the walls. In doing this, she barked her knuckles several times and once gave her head such a bump that she thought she would faint. The only thing to do, she discovered, was to press on, existing from moment to moment and not letting her mind dwell on whatever might lie ahead.

But she could not help hearing all the time the refrain inside her head, 'My knees are turning to jelly; I'll never keep going!'

However, keep going she did and at last, after what seemed an eternity, she saw to her relief that she would have to stop for the tunnel ended in a blank wall just ahead. The relief was short-lived as it happened for there was another problem now: the tunnel had no visible means of exit and they were trapped just as surely as they had been in the shed.

Too tired to worry overmuch just then, Jandy sank down thankfully on the floor of the passage while the Jacobites held an animated discussion.

Roy had lingered far behind all this time for he had decided to cover up all traces of their journey as he went but now he came up to join them.

'I think we are safe,' he said. 'I can hear no sounds of pursuit—why do you wait here? We have little time to lose!'

For answer, Jandy merely flashed the torch round the place where they were gathered. In every direction they were surrounded by solid rock.

'There must be a hidden spring,' said Shona. 'Maybe it's all covered with earth since the tunnel hasn't been used for a long time.'

This seemed a sensible idea and so they all took turns at kicking, pushing and pressing every likely-looking bump on the rock's surface, hoping to set off some secret mechanism. But nothing budged.

'What about the roof?' suggested Jandy. 'There must be a way out somewhere. No-one would make a passage this length just to come to a dead end.'

Accordingly, they all examined the roof but this proved equally hopeless. It was of pure rock, with no promising knobs or levers.

'Maybe,' Jandy then said hopelessly, 'if we all pushed together . . .' Her voice trailed off as she realized the impossibility of her own suggestion. There was no room for them all to stand together in the narrow space, far less do anything so active as heave together at the roof.

'Leave this to me,' commanded Roy. 'The lady is right but I can do this more ably on my own. Do you stand ready to support me, however.'—this last to Thomas.

So saying he stepped forward so that he was directly under the last section of rock roof and standing now for the first time upright, strained and thrust with his shoulders against the rock. The tension for the others was almost unbearable. They could not see what was happening but from the involuntary grunts uttered by Roy they could feel what effort he was expending. Having to stand by helplessly was not easy and yet to interfere would be stupid. Yet, despite all his efforts nothing moved.

After about ten minutes of this fruitless struggle, Roy staggered back and leaned against the wall of the tunnel, panting and breathless. The others stood silently by, wondering miserably what was to be done now. No-one could face the prospect of going tamely back into the arms of the soldiers, yet to wait here in this airless, rock-walled chamber was equally unalluring.

Suddenly a low burst of anger came from Roy, who had by now recovered some of his energy.

'Was it for this that we have suffered the miseries of these last months—to end up caught like rats in a trap!' he cried. 'No indeed, we shall find a way out!'

As he spoke, he thrust upward with his sgian dhu, prodding savagely at the unyielding rock. Or was it so unyielding? In one of his wild lunges the point of the weapon must have touched some hidden catch after all for the rock slab moved perceptibly.

In an instant Roy was back at work, thrusting and pushing upwards and, as Jandy held the fading beam of the torch focused on the spot where he worked, Thomas and Cailean joined in the task. It was not long before their efforts were rewarded as the whole section of the roof slowly tilted upwards and to everyone's joy they felt once more the wind and rain on their faces.

90

Unsteadily, they clambered out in turn and stood for a moment looking around them. They found they were high up in open country surrounded by rolling moors and with the first faint glimmerings of dawn beginning to lighten the eastern sky. So far as they could tell, there was no sign of road or house of any kind at hand.

Up the 'Head'

As he left the others in the shed while he set off on his lone mission up the hill, John suppressed firmly a sudden uncharacteristic longing for company and for the umpteenth time that night he began the walk along the 'bankie'. Apart from the hazards which surely awaited him on Carron Head, there were two possible danger-points on the road and he trod warily as a result.

Passing the Stewarts cottage was the first hurdle and he felt his stomach muscles contract uncomfortably in a nervous spasm when he thought for a moment that he heard a footstep behind him as he came abreast of it. Had one of the Redcoats escaped from the house and lain in wait for the first chance passer-by? Worse still, did the soldiers know somehow where he was going and were they going to try and stop him? It took him all his will-power to force himself to look round but, when he did, relief flooded through him as he saw that there was no-one there.

He went on again, faster this time and again came the soft 'slap, slap' as if there was someone, wearing loose shoes of some kind, following him. Once more he turned and strained his eyes to see but again he saw nothing. Only the darkness seemed to be pressing in around him and more menacing than before.

When he heard the sound a third time he felt he had to do something positive about it.

'I can't have this thing lurking behind me all the way up the Head,' he thought. 'Better settle it once and for all.'

He stopped and turning, retraced his steps for a short distance, trying to move as noiselessly as possible. To his bewilderment, the footfall came again—but still behind him.

It took him a few minutes to realize that the noise was made by the hood of his kagoule, flapping wetly on his back. He was wearing so many layers of clothes that he had not felt the hood being blown from his head.

'I'd better get a move on now,' he thought, 'or I'll never get the beacon lit in time. I could have done without that waste of time. I wonder what time it is. I wonder how the others are getting on up by the burn. Somebody will have to carry Robbie or the Jacobites will never see Banff tonight.'

There was so much to occupy his mind that he covered the next stretch of the way without once noticing the ruts and ridges which made the going so rough. He did not even notice the lack of a torch until, that is, he was jerked back into reality by a chilling sound. It was a long, dreadful groan and it seemed to come from just under his feet.

'Who's there?' he called, sharply he hoped although in actual fact he felt like turning tail and fleeing—anywhere away from that inhuman sound.

Whatever response he had expected, the reply he received took him by surprise.

''Tis I, Rick,' came a weak voice, tailing off in another heart-rending moan.

Until that moment, John had totally forgotten about the trooper whom Roy had left, wrapped in his plaid, in the close between the cottages. He went over cautiously towards the dreadful sounds, half-suspecting some kind of trap. Were these realistic groans just to lure him into it? No, they were too convincing and the long, shuddering breath at the end could not be mere pretence.

Without a light, John was rather handicapped in his attempts to find out what ailed the man. He had to be content with simply running his hands gently over him as he lay there by the roadside. The soldier's brow was fevered and there were patches of something warm and sticky on his head. This much John discovered without much trouble.

'Have you broken any bones, do you think?' he asked, and receiving no reply—was the man too ill to speak or did he not understand twentieth-century Scottish accents?—went on, 'I'm just going to feel your legs and arms to see if you have. I'll try not to be rough.'

Privately he was thinking what a mad business this was. He knew nothing about first aid and had never in his life before been involved in anything like this with his own contemporaries. So what help would he be, especially to a man who was not even of his own time but must have died at least two hundred years before? Yet all his instincts told him that he could not simply ignore the wounded man.

'For pity's sake, help me or I perish,' whispered the soldier, almost as if he was reading John's thoughts and he seized his arm in a grip of appeal. 'The chill is entered into my bones yet my head feels a-fevered. Canst find me one of my comrades to render me aid?'

'Sorry, old chap,' said John to himself. 'That's one thing I daren't do.' Aloud though, he answered, 'I don't know where your friends are but I will help you to reach our house, if you like. At least you will be warmer there.'

It was obviously a great effort to Rick to rise but, with help, he at last managed it. Then, leaning heavily on his

93

companion, he hobbled along to the door of No 63, where John with some difficulty supported him while he fumbled with the lock.

'Stay here by the fire,' said John, ushering him in. 'If I see any of your people I will tell them you are here. Now I must go for I have something important to do.'

There was still sufficient life in the peats to cast quite a glow over the room and John was aware of being well scrutinized by the soldier. As he turned to go, he noticed the bowl of water which Shona had used to clean Iain Ban's wound and on an impulse he emptied this at the sink and refilled it with fresh water.

'Maybe you would like to try and clean your head up while you are here,' he remarked. 'I'm sorry I can't wait.'

Feeling that he had done as much as he could for the soldier, he was on the point of leaving when a hand laid on his arm restrained him.

'I know not who you are,' muttered the Englishman, 'but methinks you know something of this.'

As he spoke, he slipped something into John's hand and he recognized with a shock of surprise the stone ball which Robbie had picked up on Gowrie beach.

As he pocketed it, he wondered momentarily just what had been the role of this stone in the night's adventures. It had kept cropping up and after all it was a link between the two centuries. But he said nothing of this to the soldier who still eyed him curiously.

'My brother will be pleased to get this back,' was all John said. 'Thank you and—good luck!'

As he closed the cottage door behind him, he paused to review his position. If Rick had been lying there undiscovered all this time there should not be much fear that he would meet any English soldiers in the village. So Ben was either skulking in the Hall afraid to emerge for fear of meeting a banshee or else he was still helplessly drunk.

'Whatever he's doing,' thought John, 'I'm not likely to see him.'

This was a comforting idea and he stepped out after that with a lighter heart. Soon he reached the base of Carron Head.

The route up the headland began in a deceptively simple way for there was a well-defined track leading between natural walls formed by waist-high rocks. So even in the darkness it was impossible for the traveller to go astray. Unfortunately this part was only about twenty yards in length and after that lay trouble.

In the carefree atmosphere of his previous climbs up 'The Head' John had made up names for the different stages just as mountaineers do for famous peaks. The beginning was 'Easy Street'.

'Now for the Nursery Slopes,' John told himself and he actually spoke out loud, for the sound of his own voice comforted him. 'Here's where we start to go up.'

In summer this was quite a pleasant stretch of firm turf on a gentle incline which was not too taxing to the lungs. Also it was from here that one had the first glimpse of the marvellous view of land and sea for which the hill was famous. Of course, tonight's weather conditions were hardly those of high summer but still John foresaw no problems. He knew the place so well—or thought he did.

Two steps were enough to tell him otherwise. How, after all, could he have known that the torrential rain of the last few hours had turned the pleasant Nursery Slopes into a sort of miniature rapids? One step, and his shoes were drenched; two steps, and his feet were swept away from him and he was left floundering on his hands and knees in the water.

In a second he was on his feet again but he was not quite so sprightly as he continued up the slope. For one thing it was not so easy to walk with soggy, sodden feet and for another the sudden fall had dampened his spirits as well as his clothes and he was wondering, not for the first time, if the whole project was really worthwhile.

'How much,' he thought, 'can anything I do tonight affect the fate of people living more than two hundred years ago? Can my actions really save them? Or am I just kidding myself that this is important?'

The whole problem was too difficult for him and he determinedly put it out of his mind. Strangely enough however he never once seriously considered giving up the climb and despite the difficulties his pace never slackened. In fact, he had been so busy thinking about the whole puzzling affair that he had reached the end of the Nursery Slopes and was well up the Screes without noticing what he was doing.

'Help,' he said aloud when he realized where he was, 'I should have been thinking more about what I'm doing and less about why I'm doing it. If I slip here, I'll go helter-skelter straight down to the rocks below.'

The Screes were the most dangerous section of the hill for this was where the slope was steepest and its danger increased by the loose stones littered all over it. Perhaps because he had been preoccupied, John had not lost his footing once until now but as so often happens the moment he began to think about what he was doing, he found himself slithering about helplessly. In the end he decided to forget his dignity and cover the remainder of the Screes on his hands and knees.

He accomplished this fairly easily but at some cost to his knees. The only thing that worried John, who was not over-careful about his appearance, was that the holes in his trousers now let in an uncomfortable draught.

'Still,' he comforted himself, 'the next bit is the Whinny Knowes and that's more sheltered.'

He plunged thankfully on to Stage Four. Here there was a

series of humps and hillocks, dotted all over with whin bushes. In summer their cheerful, yellow blossoms made a grand splash of colour but the unwary received many a scratch from the wicked prickles hidden among the bright, green foliage. Now John was to discover that in Autumn when the leaves had withered and the thorns dried out, their stab was even more painful.

'At least I can see where I'm going a bit better,' he told himself, '—not that it's doing me much good!' he added ruefully as he disentangled himself from the jagged grasp of yet another bush.

As he got rid of that one another branch whipped across his face and left it stinging.

'Oh, let me out of this,' groaned John. 'That last one nearly got me in the eye and I don't want to risk that even for the Jacobites!'

Luckily, it was not long afterwards that he emerged on to the last, although not the least testing, part of his journey. Here at the top of the climb the slope levelled off somewhat and the only vegetation was the strong, wiry grass which seemed positively to thrive in the inhospitable climate up there—anything taller would have been literally blown away by the force of the wind which now, as so often, was battering the cliff-face with all the untrammeled fury which it had stored up on its journey across the open sea.

But the very openness of the summit held its own perils for the unwary as John soon discovered.

'Crikey!' He felt the exclamation spring involuntarily to his lips when the gale caught him by the throat as he stepped from the comparative shelter of the whins. He actually heard nothing however for the sound of his voice was lost amid the turmoil of the storm. Not for nothing had he christened this part 'The Last Gasp', John reflected. If the struggle up the hill had not robbed you of your last breath, it would be whipped away by the wind at the top.

'Who would have thought you could be suffocated by the fresh air?' he wondered, striving to maintain his precarious stance on a slippery outcrop of rock. Then he amended the question to himself: 'Of course, who would have believed that air could be as fresh as this? It quite takes my breath away!'

He found himself giggling helplessly at this very weak joke and took himself sternly to task for losing control.

'A fat lot of good you'll do the Jacobite cause if you allow yourself to go off your head all on your own up here without even having lit the signal fire first. These people are depending on you, you know.'

Making heroic efforts to concentrate his mind on his task, he began very cautiously to familiarise himself with the ground in his immediate vicinity. It would be too bad if a hasty step too near the cliff-edge should cause him to stumble over the brink and send him plunging down to— but at that point he pulled his thoughts to order once more.

'What's the good of being morbid?' he asked himself. 'Think about what might happen and you'll very likely make it happen! Now you've got to decide what's the best spot for the beacon if it's to be seen in Banff. So stand still and take stock!'

Resolutely bracing himself to withstand the elements while he found his bearings, he peered out to sea. Was Big Roy perhaps doing the same, taking a last look at the land which he was soon to leave and might in all probability never see again? John thought it very likely.

One thing puzzled him: his view was naturally limited by the darkness, although there were faint signs in the sky that dawn was approaching. However, there should have been all the lights of Porterfield across the bay and of Banff in the distance but there was nothing.

'That's queer,' he mused. 'Don't tell me I really am back in Jacobite times now, before the invention of electricity! If that's the case, how do I get back to my own age?'

Suddenly he remembered the power failure during the storm. It must have been a general fault.

'Thank goodness for that,' John said. 'Now for the beacon.'

It would have been quite impossible to light a fire out there on the open headland but all along John had had a half-formed plan at the back of his mind just in case this should be so. There was a small cave on the sea-ward side of the headland, just below the crest. Any fire lit there would surely be visible from across the water and the task of lighting it would be made easier by the shelter the cave would afford.

This part of the expedition went like clockwork. John carefully lowered himself over the top of the hill and slowly worked his way over to where he thought the cave should be. He found it without difficulty and crept inside. Once there, it was the work of minutes to pile up enough debris left by summer visitors to make a good-sized bonfire. Then he took out the box of matches which he had kept stowed in an innermost pocket for safety's sake. Soon the dry brushwood was alight and the flames quickly licked their way up over the whole pile. John threw some more pieces of wood on top and then made his way out again.

'Funny thing is,' he told himself, 'I'll probably never know whether or not the right people saw the fire.'

For several reasons he had decided to try to rejoin the rest of his party by going along the high ground instead of going down the hill again and through the village. It was not an easy journey but at least it had no hazards quite so frightening as the 'Last Gasp'. After ten minutes or so, John stopped for a breather and despite the wetness of the ground threw himself down on the turf to rest.

Idly, he looked out to sea again and was astonished to see in the distant blackness a fire suddenly leap up as if in answer to his. A warm feeling of satisfaction spread through him at the sight and this remained with him until, by a lucky chance, he met up with the others just as they were standing in an undecided huddle by the tunnel exit.

The Morning After

After the long experience of darkness in the tunnel, Jandy found that even the little lightening in the sky was enough to let her see quite well. To her surprise she found that she recognized the spot where they stood. They were at a favourite summer-time picnic spot, marked by a small stone cairn. This now lay, a tumbled heap, near the open tunnel entrance. No wonder the trap-door had been so hard to shift—the cairn must have been built on top of it!

Jandy turned to mention her discovery to John but remembered with disappointment that he was not with them.

'I can't even worry about him,' she thought in surprise. 'There have been so many frights tonight that my nerves have gone numb.'

It was Robbie who saw the travel-stained figure come tramping over the moor towards them.

'Hallo,' he called. 'Look everybody. Here's John!'

They had so much to tell one another that the first moments of the reunion were mainly taken up with incoherent chatter. John was fascinated by the tale of the secret passage and wanted to know all about it. At the same time he was bursting with his own adventures and insisted on recounting them.

But after the first excitement was spent, an awkward silence fell. There was a decided feeling of anti-climax now that the dangerous part of the project was past. The Jacobites were well on the way to Banff and the boat which would take them to freedom in France on the morning tide. But what of the Turnbulls?

They suddenly realized that they were miles from home, in the middle of the night and that a typical late October drizzle was just beginning to fall.

'We must find somewhere to shelter till morning,' John decided, 'and then we'll try to get back down to Gowrie. Maybe things will be back to normal by then.' He did not specify what 'things'.

Jandy nodded. 'Back to normal' was what she craved to be above all else. She restrained herself from voicing the nagging fears that it might still be the eighteenth century down in Gowrie.

Judging their best way to travel from the position of the sea, the group set off again. They had not gone far when they came upon a big barn which was obviously used for storing peats. Thankfully the children stumbled in, the two youngest being already asleep on the backs of their long-suffering bearers. When set down, each of them instinctively found a comfortable spot and, without opening their eyes, fell again into a deep slumber.

Jandy remained conscious just long enough to shake their Highland friends warmly by the hand and to wish them good luck on their journey. Then even she succumbed to weariness and simply had to close her eyes—only for a minute. She slept.

So only John was left to observe the four Jacobites slip quietly out on to the moor again, to be lost to view in minutes in the early morning mist. Then John too slept.

Suddenly he was brought back to consciousness by a hand grasping his arm and a voice speaking urgently in his ear, 'Just tell me,' it said and John realized that it was Roy who spoke and in some excitement. 'I know now that you are not of our time and so you must have the answer. Does the King come into his own again? Does our Prince win in the end?'

Sadly, John shook his head, glad that the darkness spared him the sight of the Jacobite's eager face.

'No,' he whispered. 'I'm afraid not—but everyone in our time supports Bonnie Prince Charlie.'

A despairing groan was the Highlander's response to this.

'Mo chridhe, mo chridhe!' he moaned. 'I had the feeling that it was hopeless.'

At this, he rose and stepped through the door and soon he too had gone for ever.

*　　*　　*　　*　　*

Jock Smith, the commercial traveller in animal foodstuffs, had had a busy time lately. On Friday he came up by train from Edinburgh to Aberdeen where, immediately on arrival, he went off to hire a car. Then he booked in at a hotel for the night, telling the manager that he wanted an early call the following day.

On Saturday he was out on the doorstep at five in the morning ready to start his day's rounds, with nothing inside him but a strictly unofficial cup of tea coaxed out of the porter. That whole day he toured farms in the area, reaching as far afield as Banff. There a kindly farmer's wife insisted that he would stay for the night.

'The trouble with this kind of hospitality,' reflected Jock as he was awakened next morning by the unmusical sound of clanking pails, 'is that they feed you too well and wake you too early.'

Now that he was awake, however, he decided to get up and make an early start for his base in Aberdeen. He could always take it easy in the hotel for the rest of the day.

The morning was dull and mist hung everywhere as he drove through the dank countryside and the traveller would have given much to have had a car radio or cassette player—anything to provide diversion. However he had to make do with his own singing.

'Yellow submarine!' he yelled as he negotiated the quiet roads, not being very well up on the latest pop. Then he broke off and braked wildly in astonishment.

Drawn up in an orderly fashion by the roadside was a familiar-looking little group. Surely he had come across them somewhere before? A big boy, a tall girl and a small boy and girl and, yes, a black and white cat and a shaggy Scottie dog. Of course, these were the kids from the train. Watching them and listening to their conversation had fairly shortened the journey for him.

Jock stopped his car and stepped out.

'Hallo,' he called. 'What in the name of all that's weird and wonderful are you doing here?'

'That man was on the train!' cried Shona excitedly. 'Oh, thank goodness, it's just an ordinary man.'

The traveller had no time to question the meaning of this extraordinary greeting, however, for he was immediately assailed by questions and comments on all sides.

'Stop!' he commanded, hands to ears. 'Stop and wheesht! It's no use all talking at once.'

He turned to John, as the eldest.

'Can you tell me what's up?' he asked.

'Well,' replied John slowly. 'Yes and no. We've got a very queer story to tell and you may hardly believe it. What we'd really like, though, is to get back down to our house at Gowrie. There was a landslide in the storm last night and we're not sure if the road's open. Could you possibly give us a lift?'

'Surely,' said Jock agreeably. 'Hop in but mind your dog doesn't jump on the car seats. It's only a hire.'

The children piled in thankfully, Jandy in front with Robbie on her knee and John, Shona and Hamish behind. Tibby, when they looked round for her, was nowhere to be seen. In spite of Robbie's protests, they had to set off without her.

'She'll find her own way home,' said John. 'She knows the countryside better than any of us.'

'And now,' said the traveller after introducing himself, 'what's this great story of yours?'

Half an hour later as they turned down Gowrie Brae, he was beginning to revise his earlier good opinion of the Turnbulls.

'They're clean daft,' he thought, 'and I imagined they were such a cheery crowd.'

'It certainly sounds an incredible story,' John was thinking, 'but he did ask for it!'

The road was quite clear this morning and the car was able to take them all the way to the parking place where there was a small group of people gathered. Some of them were evidently churchgoers who could not take their usual Sunday morning stroll over to Porterfield but others were just there to exchange storm stories. Among these was Mrs Wood who detached herself from the crowd and came hurrying over when she saw the children.

'Am I glad to see you!' she cried. 'Whatever became of you last night? Have you seen the damage in all the houses— just terrible to think what a night of storm can do!'

'That was partly why we left,' Jandy told her. 'We were afraid the whole hillside behind us was going to come down on the house. Is it badly damaged, do you know?'

104

'Bad enough,' returned Mrs Wood, 'but nothing to the broken windows and burst doors at the front. You could hardly believe the weather could do such damage; it looks more like the work of vandals!'

John and Jandy exchanged knowing looks. It was the work of vandals, they were thinking, but of vandals who lived two hundred years ago and more.

Just then a small black and white figure appeared, leaping down from the rocks to join the group. Robbie let out a cry of delight and rushed forward.

'Tibby, my wee pea-jack!' he cried. 'Where have you come from?'

The Highland policeman who had come to inspect the effects of the storm smiled at this reunion.

'So it's a "piseag" is it?' he grinned. 'And where did you pick up the Gaelic, mo laochain?'

'Pea-jack, that's what Iain Ban called her,' said Robbie. 'So I'm going to call her Tibby Pea-jack now.'

Jock Smith looked as if he could not believe the evidence of his own ears.

'The sooner I get out of this mad-house, the better,' he muttered, climbing hastily into his car. 'These kids are not canny.'

He drove smartly off and when he reached his hotel he went to bed for the rest of the afternoon just in case he had been suffering from the effects of working too hard.

As for the children, they were only too glad to get back to No. 63—a sadly battered cottage now, to be sure, but one that meant home and comfort and safety to them none the less. Mrs Wood fussed around them in a very agreeable way and even Jandy was only too pleased to sit back and accept gratefully all she was offered.

They slept soundly all morning and, by the time they had risen and had some lunch, the first effects of their busy night

105

were already beginning to disappear.

At one point in the afternoon, as they sat watching the lobstermen from the jetty, Jandy turned to John.

'What do you think really happened last night?' she asked. 'How did we get mixed up in all that?'

'I've been trying to decide that myself,' returned her brother. 'All I can think is that it must be partly because of Robbie's stone for that was the connection with the Jacobites and partly because of the landslide for that made—'

'It made Gowrie Head reach Gowrie shore,' finished Jandy. 'That rhyme kept running through my head last night and to think that we said it was impossible!'

John nodded.

'It just goes to show that you can never be sure of anything,' he said sagely.

'There's one thing I will say and that is: if Robbie picks up any more ancient objects from the beach, I'll throw them straight back into the water before there's any more funny business.'

'Still, it's something to talk about,' was John's comment.

Oddly enough, that was not quite true. They certainly tried to talk about their adventure but people reacted so strangely that they soon gave up. However there was one postscript to the story which only came out about a year later.

John came into the living-room at home one night in a state of great excitement. Jandy was alone in the room and was not at all pleased when her brother not only interrupted the programme she was watching but actually switched off the set without so much as a by-your-leave.

'What do you think—!' she began indignantly but her brother ignored her angry exclamation.

'Just listen!' he said. 'I've found out something really interesting.'

He told her that he had been down at the library where he

106

had noticed a Gaelic dictionary. Idly browsing through it, he had come upon a list of surnames at the back and had decided to look for the name 'Turnbull', to see if it had a Gaelic equivalent. He did not find it but as it happened, he discovered something more unusual.

'It was the name MacIan,' said John. 'You know, the name of our Jacobites. Can you guess what it is in English?'

'Yes,' answered Jandy, with a trace of impatience. 'It's Johnston. I thought you would have realized that. Everyone knows that "mac" means "son of" and Iain is the same as John.'

'So do you mean to tell me that you knew all along that Big Roy was the husband of Mary Johnston?'

'Of course,' his sister replied calmly. 'He was our great-great umpteen times grandfather. It never occurred to me that you would have to be told. Now, can I watch my film again?'

John's exasperation at this cool reception of his amazing discovery was tremendous. Still, it only confirmed what he had always suspected—sisters were a funny lot!